GOLDEN DERRINGERS

GOLDEN DERRINGERS

J.E. GRINSTEAD

ILLUSTRATED BY
SAMUEL CAHAN

COVER BY
PAUL STAHR

POPULAR PUBLICATIONS · 2022

TABLE OF CONTENTS

GOLDEN DERRINGERS

*Pushing north with a thousand
steers, young Price Stanley runs into
a grim mystery of the Ozarks*

1

NATURAL ENEMIES

SCUFFING THROUGH THE shinnery and camphor weed, on either side of the worn old trail, a herd of cattle was beating steadily north through the Ozark hills, toward the Missouri prairies. They were following what was known as the Red Road, which was the old stage road that led from Arrow Rock, on the Missouri River, to Fort Smith, Arkansas.

The men driving that herd were not called trail drivers, but cattle drovers. They were, however, the same hardy breed of men who wrote the romance of cattle in the old West. This herd was considerably ahead of the first herd of Texas cattle that came that way, but there was something still ahead of it that was likely to make trouble.

On a cross trail, going east toward the Paramo River, half a dozen men were driving a little band of scrawny stock cattle. Before they realized what was happening to them, a thousand beef steers swept over and around the little herd, and they were lost. The hill men, who had been driving the little herd, came storming back to the drovers, cursing and threatening as they came. Several of the drovers halted in a little knot.

"What's troubling you hill-billies?" demanded lank, flat-cheeked, bewhiskered old Dave Baker.

"Why, they's plenty pestering us," snarled one of the men. "You damn' cattle drovers think you own the Red Road. I'll tell you a few things. I'll tell you who I am. I'm Sile Perkins, of Rollin' Fork, over east, beyond the river. Another thing I aim to tell you is that they can't nary damn' cattle drover that ever popped a whup run it over me."

"Well, what are you going to do about it?" grinned old Dave, who would rather fight than eat. "How do you want to do it, on yo' horse, with a gun, on the ground with yo' fists? Name the way you want to commit suicide, and let's go."

"On the ground, with fists, like men," snarled Mr. Perkins, sliding from his saddle, and his men following him.

"Come on, boys!" yelled Dave. "There's only five of us, but we can trim six hill-billies."

Dave and his companions were dismounting and preparing for battle, when a big Kentucky saddler came charging through the shinnery from the other side of the old trail. It was a fine-looking horse, and on it was a fine-looking man. He was a young fellow, still in his twenties, but he was not a boy just then. His hair was raven black, and his dark eyes flashed. He was over six foot, and didn't look it. His handsome face was hard and stern as he pulled up his horse and called:

"What's going on here, Dave?"

"I don't know," grinned Dave Baker. "These billies want to fight, and we aim to please."

"Get back on your horses. Now, if you gentlemen have any cause for complaint, I'm the man you want to talk to."

"An' I'll damn' shore talk," snarled Perkins. "I'm drivin'

Old Dave strode toward the snarling hill-
billies, his fists clenched

some cattle acrost this here trail, an' yo' herd just runs over 'em, an' sops 'em up, like a biscuit in the gravy pan. You cattle drovers think you own the earth. You don't think anythin' of takin' a widder woman's milk calves an' cows. You'd steal—"

"That will do from you," said the big herd-boss. "If your cattle are in this herd, we'll get them out for you as soon as we come to some open ground. This outfit is not stealing cattle from anybody."

"Your outfit ain't no different from any other cattle drovers. They'll all steal anythin' they can lay their hands on, and then back it up with guns. I know 'em, and—"

"Shut up, and get on your horses!" snapped the boss. "Stop the cattle in the first open place you come to, boys, and if any of you start a fight you'll have to settle with me."

Price Stanley whirled the big saddler and dashed away to the head of the herd. The cattle were stopped, and a few minutes later Mr. Silas Perkins and his men were hazing their band of scrawny cattle on east through the shinnery.

"PRICE," SAID OLD Dave Baker, dropping back by the

side of the boss as the herd started on, "what made you take that talk off'n that hill-billy? Yo' daddy will be ashamed of you if he ever finds that out."

"My daddy holds me responsible for these steers," said Price, "and I mean to keep them moving. I have no time to stop and thrash a hill-billy. Not only that, I have an idea that these hill folks have a real grievance against cattle drovers. Some of them are a pretty tough lot."

"Well, I don't take no talk off'n 'em. If you'd let me—"

"As long as you are working for me, Dave, do what I tell you to do. When we get these cattle home, if you want to you can draw your pay, come back here, and whip as many hill-billies as you like—or get beat to death by them."

"I'd like to see one of 'em beat me to death!"

"Yes, I think I'd rather enjoy that myself, but not just now. Take the herd, keep it moving, and keep out of trouble. I'm going on ahead to find a place to pen the cattle for the night. I think we'll put up at the old Vane House, a short distance this side of Vaneburg."

Price Stanley rode around the herd and took the road on ahead. As he went along he thought things over. His father, old Banks Stanley, had been a soldier in Price's Army, in the war between the States. The fall of Appomattox did not break the elder Stanley's spirit, as it did the spirit of many. He had simply gone back to his big farm on the Missouri prairies and set about making another fortune.

To do this he drove cattle from the Missouri-Arkansas line, up through the Ozarks, before ever Mr. Chisholm had blazed his famous trail from Texas. Banks Stanley had grown old in the game, and now Price was making his first trip as boss in his father's stead.

These cattle drovers wore no chaps nor broad hats, and carried no lassos. They drove cattle with long-lash, short-handled whips, which were coiled at the saddlehorn when not in use, much the same as a cowboy carries his rope. This outfit which Price Stanley was bossing would have been a joke to a Texas trail outfit. The men were not cowboys, but looked more like a gang of farm hands riding plow horses. The boss of such an outfit could always be distinguished from his men by the fact, that instead of a plug he rode a thoroughbred Kentucky saddler.

The cattle were gentle, having been raised in milk pens by the Ozark mountaineers, and were hazed quietly along the old Red Road.

Price and his men had never heard of such a thing as night herding. They could not conceive of a herd that could not be penned at night in some farmer's clover patch.

Young Stanley swung on down the Red Road toward the crossing on the Paramo River. He knew nothing of the Vane House and its occupants; but his father had told him Captain Vane had a clover pasture that he rented to drovers, and that it would be a good place to pen the herd for a night on the drive.

There was no thought that he was riding toward adventure, as the big saddler swiftly covered the five miles from where the hill-billies had tried to make trouble, to the grim old stone building.

THE OLD VANE HOUSE fronted on the Red Road. The road was not actually red at that point. It was called the Red Road because an army had once retreated over it and the soil had been dyed with blood. Also because, when the war was over, the old road became a cattle trail and the drovers dyed it with some more blood. In the old stage days, passengers often asked the driver about that old stone house, as they passed it, and the driver would say:

"That's the old Vane place. Old Cap'n Franklin Vane, his wife, and his—granddaughter, I reck'n—lives thar. They are the last of the Vanes, to anybody's knowin'."

It was a squat, one-story stone building, as it appeared from the road, standing gray and grim, well back in a grove of ancient oak, walnut and elm trees, many of which were overgrown with ivy. It was built at the top edge of the bluff, and was two stories at the back, the lower story being carved out of the bluff.

The back yard, with its old stone spring-house, was a shelf or terrace of the bluff. From the back yard gate a flight of stone steps led down to another level, on which stood Vane's Mill. The old mill, once a flourishing flour mill with a woolen mill adjoining, had been silent for years. Its broken waterwheel was overgrown with vines and ferns.

The old Vane House was more than spooky. It had the very air of tragedy about it. It was a bit of the Old World, transplanted to bustling western America, and then forgotten. It was a fine Western joke that such a place should be on a cattle trail. It was not so much that bodies had perished there, and had been laid to molder in graves. That happens everywhere. There was something about the house that indicated that souls had died there, and the grim tenements of flesh had gone on living, aimlessly.

About two o'clock in the afternoon, old Captain Franklin Vane crossed the terraced back yard, with a can of bait in his hand. The captain, a tall, spare man, who rarely spoke, was past seventy, and his hair and beard were snowy white.

His right shoulder was slightly drooped, because a Minié ball had wrecked the right lung, at Missionary Ridge.

Out the back gate and down the steps to the mill level, the captain took his way cautiously. Then he stood as straight as his infirmities would permit, while he crossed the mill yard. He loved the gray, broken old mill, because it had once been the glory of the Vanes. On past the mill, the old man clambered down other steps, which were now broken in many places.

At the foot of these, he stopped on a big, flat rock. It was the captain's favorite fishing place. Just where the water still came out of the old millrace, gurgled through the broken wheel, and formed a small, deep hole below it.

Captain Vane baited two hooks, as was his custom. One fish pole he set in a crevice in the rocks, while he held the other in his hand. Thus he would sit, for hours at a time, his pipestem held insecurely in his broken teeth, and watch the two bobbers in the little blue pool.

The cork on the one he held in his hand began to bob. He jerked skillfully, and not too hard. The cork shot to the bottom of the pool. The captain pulled out a nice channel cat, and stooped over to take it from the hook.

That was the last fish for Captain Franklin Vane. He clutched his left breast, fell over, rolled off the big rock into the blue pool, and clutched at some timbers of the broken water-wheel. For a moment he kept his head above water, and stared about him. Then slowly he sank. His white beard spread upon the water, and next his hair, there was a gurgle, and he was gone.

No, not gone, exactly. The left hand had caught in the

crotch of some timbers, just above the water line, one long, bony finger pointing accusingly across the river.

WATER GURGLED ON through the broken mill wheel and the little pool, finding its way back to the river from which it had come at a natural fall above the mill. It seemed to have changed its merry tune to a question: "Why, why, why?" as it passed on its way into the Paramo.

Even the river's name was as strange in that country as was Vane's Mill. Some intrepid explorer from the early colony about Saint Louis had wandered up that stream and found a wilderness and biting cold. He may have been a Frenchman, but he knew his Spanish, so he called the river Paramo; a wilderness; a cold place.

Mrs. Matilda Vane was a product of Kentucky's ante-bellum days. In her girlhood she had been the toast of half a dozen counties in the blue-grass section. She had borne no child, and now, nearing three-score, she was still graceful and lovely. With a wealth of snowy hair that set like a crown on her shapely head.

The dashing captain had married her in war time, before he was wounded. After the war, he brought her a bride to the old Vane House. True to the tenets of her faith and the custom of the day, she had lived her life there. That is, her graceful body had lived. Her spirit was long since broken and her soul dead.

Long before night Mrs. Vane began going to the back window and peering out and down across the terraced yard and on to the mill. She knew the captain was growing feeble with age. Once, when he failed to come in before sunset, she had gone to seek him. He had not railed at her, for he was a gentleman, but she had never sought him again.

THE RED ROAD ran north for a quarter mile, then circled east through the bottom, to cross the Paramo over the old covered bridge. Just beyond the Vane House on the left was a gate leading into a forty-acre clover meadow. Many a drove of cattle had spent a night on that meadow, at so much per head. That was one of Captain Vane's principal sources of income.

So it happened that Price Stanley, twenty-eight, tall, dark, with flashing black eyes, reined his Kentucky saddler at the Vane yard gate, dismounted, removed his tiny brass spurs, and went to the gray old house. He had never been there before, but he knew the place, and his father had told him of Captain Vane and his clover field.

Stanley entered the wide portico and knocked at the door. It was opened presently, but not by Captain Vane, as he had expected. Instead, a tall, willowy, golden-haired girl, with great, wide blue eyes, stood before him. His hat came off and he stammered:

"Good evening, ma'am—miss. Is Captain Vane in the house?"

"No, sir, he isn't," replied Myra Vane. "He went fishing, but—"

"I wanted to see him about penning my cattle in his clover field for the night. They're only a mile back the road, and I'd like—"

"Why, grandfather is only down at the mill," she replied. "I'll show you the way. Just come in."

Stanley entered the house and followed her through the wide hall, then down a flight of steps and out into the terraced back yard. The girl was leading the way, and had not spoken, until they reached the big flat rock below the old mill wheel, and then:

"Why, that's strange! There are grandfather's poles and lines, his can of bait, and there's his pipe on the rock. He must—" She broke off with a wild scream and stood pointing in wide-eyed terror at that hand with its accusing finger, caught in the timbers of the broken mill wheel.

"Oh, get him out! Get him out!" she cried.

"I—I'm afraid I can't do that alone, miss," replied Stanley. "Anyway, he is quite dead, and we should have an officer—"

"Come on, then. Let's go tell grandmother."

They hurried back through the mill yard. Mrs. Vane saw them from the window as they crossed the terraced back yard, and read the tragedy in their faces. In the hall she met them calmly. The Berkeleys of Kentucky didn't give way to emotions, and she was a Berkeley.

"Terrible!" she said, in a cold, strained voice, when Myra told of the horror. "I knew the captain was growing feeble, and was afraid he would fall. Who are you, young man?"

"Price Stanley," he replied. "I wanted to pen some cattle in—"

"Ah! Sterling Price, I suppose. You must be of the right sort of people. You think there should be an officer? Anyway, we must have help. Would you ride over to Vaneburg and tell the constable and justice of the peace to come over?"

"Gladly," said Stanley, but he was still thinking of those thousand cattle. The head of this exceptionally large herd, for that trail, was in sight when he stepped out the front door. He looked back at the snowy-haired chatelaine with a question in his eyes.

"Yes, you may pen your cattle on the clover," she said, "but hurry with the officers, please."

Stanley called to his men to pen the cattle, then tore away toward the old covered bridge and Vaneburg, which was just across the river, at the end of the bridge.

PRICE STANLEY HAD crossed that old bridge a good many times, and had looked at the dead old town, but it had never before looked to him just as it looked now. Coming to it as he did, fresh from a scene of tragedy, the decaying town took on a ghostly look in the gathering dusk of evening.

The road turned north at the east end of the bridge and followed what had once been the principal business street of the town. There was nothing to the left of the road but a blacksmith shop and some broken ruins of brick and stone. Of a score or more of brick and stone buildings that had once formed the business heart of a considerable village, a dozen were still standing, but most of them were tottering to fall. The glass was gone from them and the broken windows had the vacant stare of the blind.

A block from the end of the bridge a wide street ran east up the slope to what had once been the residence section. It was now a cluster of weather-beaten, ramshackle ruins. On the slope between the business section and the cluster of houses on the hill, a forest of gaunt chimneys pointed like dead fingers toward heaven. These were grim reminders, in spite of the passing years, that a fleeing army had once passed that way and had used the torch freely.

There was but one business house now occupied. That

was at the corner of Main Street and Broad Street. There was not even a saloon. Adam March, a dour, sallow-faced, saturnine man, whose eyes were black and cheek bones prominent, had a "pint license" and kept a barrel or two of forty-rod in the back of his store.

Mr. March was standing at the front of his store.

"Can you tell me where I'll find the justice of the peace?" asked Stanley.

"Over thar," growled March, and pointed across to the other street corner.

Price rode "over thar" and dismounted. He entered what had once been a store. In one corner, at the front, was a table, two chairs, and a shelf containing half a dozen law books.

Across in the other front corner, by a window, a man with abundant white beard, stooped shoulders and a peg leg, sat on a bench, skillfully pegging on a boot sole. He looked up, and Price saw that he had kindly blue eyes.

"Yes, I'm the justice," he replied to Stanley's question. "What can I do for you, young man?"

"Captain Vane has been drowned, and Mrs. Vane wants you to bring the constable and a doctor and come to the house."

"What? Captain Vane drowned? Too bad, too bad! I'll be ready to go in a few minutes, sir."

IF THE JUDGE had any other name than Peg Short, no one in that country knew it. He got about surprisingly well on that peg leg. In a very few minutes he had crossed the street, routed out Malvin Tebo, the blacksmith, who was also constable.

Together, they found Dr. Potts, a wheezy, fat old fellow,

who had been practicing along that river for years and was coroner for the township. The three piled into the doctor's crazy old phaëton, and started for the scene of the tragedy.

Mal Tebo, the constable, had brought along a boat hook, which was the only useful thing Stanley could see as he rode along behind the rickety vehicle. They all three seemed to be talking at once, but Stanley could hear nothing as they rattled across the bridge. On the other side, when the noise stopped, he heard Judge Peg Short say:

"It ain't suicide, boys. Cap'n Vane was a Christian gentleman, and—"

"Of course not!" wheezed Dr. Potts. "I've been tellin' the cap'n for a year that his heart was bad, and he smoked too much. He just tuckered out and fell in."

"By heck, I reckon we'll find out, mebbe, when we get him out'n the water!" opined Mal Tebo, as he spat a flood of tobacco juice over the wheel. Mal was a giant. He was constable because he could whip, in fact had whipped, every man in the township who would fight him.

Arrived at the scene of the tragedy, Mal caught his boat hook in the captain's garments and pulled up. The dead arm, being now stiff, the hand was raised from the fork of the timbers, and they pulled the body ashore and laid it on the big, flat rock.

"This is as far as we ought to move it, I reckon," said Judge Short, "until the coroner examines it."

"H'm, h'm, h'm!" grunted the wheezy little doctor, as he bent to his task. "What's this? H'm! Hole in the front of his shirt." The doctor opened the shirt front. "H'm! Bullet, square through the brisket. Turn him over. H'm, here it is, right under the skin at his back." There was a flick of a lancet, and the bullet was in the doctor's hand. "Take it, Peg. You may need it for evidence, I don't. My verdict is death from a gunshot, fired by some party or parties unknown. If you want a coroner's jury, you can get one, but that's the verdict you'll get."

"Then I reckon we can move him on to the house," said Peg Short.

"Yes, but I don't see how we'll pack him."

"I'll manage that," said Mal Tebo. "He's a little wet, but I don't mind."

PICKING THE DEAD man up as if he had been a little child, he climbed the broken steps and strode on to the house. Mrs. Vane had been trying to comfort Myra, who had collapsed in her room after the first shock and full realization that her grandfather was dead. Matilda Vane, with the true Berkeley calm, now showed the men where to lay the body. Dr. Potts took charge of preparing it for burial, while Peg Short helped him. Neither of them mentioned the bullet wound to Mrs. Vane. Time enough for that, when things settled a bit.

It had grown quite dark by this time. Price Stanley had ridden all day with his cattle, and in spite of the tragedy and excitement, he wanted to go to his camp and eat. More than that, he wanted his Kentucky saddler fed.

"Gentlemen," he said, "if there is anything more that I can do, I'll gladly do it. If not, I'll go on to my camp. It's just this side of the bridge. If you want me for anything, you'll find me there."

No one said anything, so Price walked out the front door, but Constable Mal Tebo walked out with him. Halfway to the gate, Mal said:

"Wait a minute. I aim to arrest you for killin' Cap'n Vane."

"Arrest me? You're crazy. I never saw Captain Vane in my life until we pulled him out of the water."

"Says you! How'n heck did you know he was in thar, then? What made you say he was drowned, instead of tellin' the truth and sayin' he was shotten? That's jes' like a damn' cattle drover. They'll do anythin'. I—"

Mal Tebo stopped, for reasons. The chief reason was that a fist as hard as iron had caught him on the button, and he was trying to distinguish the different kinds of birds that were singing. He woke up after a while, but Price Stanley was gone.

2

A FAMILY SECRET

ONLY FOUR PERSONS in the world knew that a bullet had passed through the body of the late Captain Franklin Vane. That a bullet had caused the old soldier's death, and not drowning. The caliber of the bullet was small, and there was no blood on the exterior of the body.

Mrs. Vane brought out the full regimental uniform of an officer in J.E.B. Stuart's cavalry. It was somewhat worn and faded, but she wanted the captain buried in his uniform. So, Captain Benjamin Franklin Vane, who had escaped the storms of battle and the dangers of bivouac, to be laid low by an assassin's bullet, began his last long sleep in his beloved gray uniform.

Having finished their task, Doc Potts and Peg Short stood looking down at the still form on the improvised bier.

"He was right smart of a man," said the doctor musingly.

"As brave and true and square as God in His wisdom ever created," said Judge Short reverently. "Doc, who fired that shot?"

"I been wonderin' about that myself, Peg. It looks damned strange that nobody heard it!"

"Yes, it does, but— Where's Mal Tebo?"

"He went out with that cattle drover, and— There he is now, comin' in."

"He—he got clean away!" blurted the big constable, rubbing his sore chin.

"Who got away?" demanded Short.

"Why, the damn' cattle drover. I tried to arrest him, and—"

"Well, what happened?"

"Peg, it doesn't seem possible. Nobody ever done the like before, but—that big drover knocked me cold as a wedge with his fist. He must of had knucks."

"Yeah," drawled Doc Potts, "he had knucks! I saw 'em. They was the ones God gave him, and He gave that lad considerable breadth of shoulder and other things to back those knucks up in a fight. What did you want to arrest him for?"

"What fur? Why, look here. The cap'n's dead, ain't he? He was shotten. Them cattle drovers all pack concealed weepons. Nobody else that we know of has been about this place with ary gun. I reckon I better go get my revolver, and take that feller. He's dangerous bad."

"Just a minute, Mal," said Judge Peg. "You better keep away from that camp. You go get into a mess with them drovers, and you'll last about as long as a tadpole in a duck trough. Let's find out what Mis' Vane wants did, and do it. Then we got to talk this thing over, quiet and sensible. One thing is understood: we don't mention that bullet until we know more. I wish I'd told that drover not to mention it."

"He ain't apt to mention it," said Mal Tebo. "When a feller shoots a man, he don't usually go round talkin' about it."

Mrs. Vane was consulted. No, she didn't want any of the neighbor women. If one or two men would sit in the library and keep watch, she would stay with Myra and try to console her. By morning she would decide what to do. That was all. She went to another part of the house.

"Doc," said Judge Peg, "I got to start some sort of investigation of this mess. If you'll stay here, Mal and me will get out and look around some."

"All right, Peg, but I want somebody to come back around one o'clock, and let me get some sleep in the shank of the night."

Peg Short and the constable left the house.

PRICE STANLEY WAS young and hot-headed. Mal Tebo's blunt and brutal charge of murder, without other warrant or evidence, except that he was a stranger and a cattle drover, had set him wild with rage in a flash. He had struck without thinking.

As he went on to his camp, he was thinking things over. No one knew better than he that cattle drovers had a most unsavory reputation. So much so that the better element of young men in the prairie country to the north hesitated to drive cattle, even at the good pay offered.

In his own outfit were men that were known to be brawlers and swaggering bullies. They had to be rough, or they couldn't stay in the game when they met up with other drovers. None of them carried side-arms in open view, but Price knew they were all armed, in spite of the drastic State law against carrying concealed weapons.

He himself had the Golden Derringers in convenient pockets. These beautiful but dangerous little weapons had been a gift from his father, Banks Stanley. They were little more than four inches long, but carried a ball of heavy caliber. Originally, they had been cap-and-ball guns, but an expert gunsmith had changed them to use short, stubby cartridges. A single shot to each. The little weapons were of the finest metal and workmanship, heavily plated with gold, and richly fretted and embossed.

When Banks Stanley had given them to Price, he had said:

"Take these, son, and when you travel, carry them; but never use them as long as you can defend yourself with your fists. They won't shoot straight ten feet, but they'll tear a man apart if he's on top of you, and gripped in your hand they are more deadly than any brass knucks. Take care of them. They cost five hundred dollars."

Price reached camp, fed his horse, and ate some supper. Then he took Dave Baker aside and talked to him. After telling Dave what had happened, but withholding any mention that Captain Vane had been shot, or of the constable's attempt to arrest him, he said:

"There seems to be no one at the place but two women, and they don't seem to have any neighbors. The doctor is there, and the old justice of the peace. I'm going back to the house and see if there is anything I can do."

"Better be careful," said Baker, who was a man of forty, and had been told by old Banks Stanley to look out for the boy on this trip. "These are queer folks in these Ozark hills. They don't like for other people to mess with their affairs, and they hate a cattle drover worse than they do the devil himself."

"Oh, I'm not going to push myself into anything. We've

got our cattle on their clover. They're in trouble. I just mean to be decent, that's all."

Price may have meant to be decent. The fact was, he was rather ashamed of his outburst against the officer and wanted to apologize to Mal Tebo, ignorant boor though Mal might be. As Price Stanley swung along on foot toward the grim old Vane House he was heading for more strange adventure and more trouble than ever he had known in his young life.

SO, IT HAPPENED that Price Stanley met Judge Peg and his constable at the yard gate, as they were leaving the old Vane House.

"I came back to see if I could do anything," Price said.

"Why, no," said Judge Peg. "They are sorta peculiar people. They didn't want nobody sent for. Doc is going to stay until after midnight. You might help me some, if you would."

"Why, certainly I will, if there's anything I can do. First, I want to apologize to the constable for striking him a while ago, but—"

"I reckon Malvin will accept the apology," drawled Judge Peg. "He was right smart ahead of the hounds. I don't want no arrestin' done in this case until I issue a warrant, but I've got to investigate. If you wouldn't mind going to my office, I'd like to talk to you, because you was the one that found the cap'n."

"Certainly I'll go."

The three climbed into the doctor's rickety old buggy, and Mal Tebo started plodding away toward Vaneburg. Price knew at that moment that he was as much under arrest as he would ever be in that case, or any other. The peg-leg justice had taken him calmly.

As they were passing the camp, Price said: "I'd like to speak to one of my men a moment, if you don't mind."

"All right, call him out and talk to him." Clearly, Judge Peg didn't mean for his man to get out and rally his band of tough drovers for a rescue. Price called Dave Baker and when the lanky, bewhiskered drover came to the buggy, he said:

"Dave, I'm going into town with the judge. I'll come back in the buggy with him, if he comes back. If I'm not back in two hours, you and the other boys bring my horse to me."

"Now, see here, Price," said Dave Baker, "I promised old man Banks that I—"

"Never mind that!" snapped Price Stanley. "I'm running this outfit. Do what you're told to do. All right, judge, drive on."

MAL TEBO CLUCKED to the old nag, and it trotted on through the long, dark, covered bridge. A few minutes later, the three sat in Judge Peg's office. It was lighted now by a smoky little coal-oil lamp, which failed to fight back the shadows in the big room. Mal Tebo sat scowling at Price in silence, as the judge began his investigation.

"Now, tell me just how you happened to be down at the mill and find Captain Vane?" Judge Peg's blue eyes had only kindness in them.

Price told him how he had gone to the house. That the young lady had taken him to the mill, and the whole story up to the time he had come for the officers.

"That's strange," said Peg, musingly. "That's the first time

I've heard of anybody bein' invited into that house, except the doctor, since Captain Franklin Vane come back from the Army."

"Yes, it's strange—if it's true," growled Mal Tebo. "They's always been something strange about that yaller-haired girl. They claim she's Benton Vane's—"

"Just a minute, Malvin," interrupted the judge. "I'll conduct the investigation. There's one formality I over-looked. What is your name?"

"My name is Sterling Price Stanley, and I was born and have spent all my life in Saline County over on the Missouri River."

"Stanley, eh? Any kin to Banks Stanley?"

"His son."

"Fine, fine! Now, we'll get somewhere. Banks Stanley's son couldn't tell anything but a straight story, if he tried. Banks Stanley and me clattered through that old covered bridge knee to knee one hot July day in '61, lookin' for some Yankees that got away from the Battle of Wilson's Creek. Ten mile north of here—we found 'em. That's where I lost my leg. But that's got nothin' to do with this case."

Judge Peg asked Price a few more questions, and then said:

"Well, that leaves us where we started, with nothin' at all to take hold of to unravel the mess. Now—"

"If I was handlin' it, I could find somethin' to take hold of mighty quick," interrupted Mal Tebo. "First thing I'd take hold of would be—"

"Never mind, Malvin. We can't take hold of anythin' to-night. There might be tracks or somethin' down about

Vane's Mill that would lead to somethin', but if we go there at night, we'll only mess things up."

"I wouldn't have to go there to get hold of—"began the constable.

"Now, Malvin," said Judge Peg, patiently, "you ain't handlin' this investigation. I'll call on you in the mornin' when I need you. Go on up to your house and go to bed. Get some sleep, so you'll be fit for trailin' the killer if we find a track when daylight comes."

Mal Tebo rose and left, but not without a scowling backward glance at Price Stanley. When Mal was gone, the judge said:

"It don't hurt a man much to be a fool, if he knows it. Malvin don't know it. Bein' elected constable because everybody in the township was afraid to run agin' him, has sorty swelled his head."

A FEW MOMENTS of silence followed. Price Stanley had nothing to say. Old Peg Short seemed casting about in his mind for a starting point.

"So, you are Banks Stanley's boy! Well, I can talk to you, and that's more than I can say for most of my neighbors. This killin' stumps me. If Cap'n Vane ever had an enemy, I never heard of it."

Old Peg Short stopped, filled a cob pipe with home-grown tobacco and went on, apparently talking to himself:

"My daddy told me about old Anson Vane, when I was a boy. He was the granddaddy of Captain Franklin Vane. Old Anson was a Virginian. One of them old silk-stocking, silver-buckle gents. He brought in a passel of niggers and started Vane's Mill.

"When old Anson died, his son, Randall Vane, took hold

and pushed on. He built the mill up to a power. People brought corn and wheat for miles around to be ground. They brought wool, too, to be spun and wove into cloth. Randall Vane was a hard driver and smart as a whip.

"Then, just at the breakin' out of the war, Randall Vane up and died, leavin' everythin' to his son, the cap'n. Cap'n Franklin Vane had married, and— Funny thing about the Vanes. They each had one son, and no more."

"Did Captain Franklin Vane have a son?" asked Price.

"Yes, he did, but— Well, it can't hurt nobody for me to tell you this. Franklin Vane went away and got him a wife. He had one son, Benton Vane. Then his wife died, just before the war.

"Franklin Vane come back from the war with one lung, a new wife, and a captain's title. Vaneburg was burned up. The mill had gone to ruin. Benton Vane was grown then, and he was a heller. He didn't hit it off with his new mammy, and soon after she came into the house, he went out and headed west. He's never been back since."

"Have they ever heard of him?" asked Price, who was becoming interested.

"Huh. More than you have asked that question. About three year after Bent Vane went away, the stage stopped at the old Vane house one day. A shut-mouthed woman, with a baby in her arms, got out and went into the house. She had come down from Arrow Rock. Next day the up stage stopped at Vane's, and the same woman got on, but she didn't have no baby!"

"Why, what became of it?"

"Well, nobody knew for a long time. Then one day, coupla years later, Franklin Vane comes into my shop to order a pair of new boots. He had a little yaller-haired girl baby with him, and he says to me, 'Peg, this is Benton's daughter.' That's the only time I ever heard him mention Benton, or the girl either. She growed up there at the Vane house. She went away to school a lot. Then she come back. She goes by the name Myra Vane, but—nobody knows anythin' about her, or why they left her with her grandfather and his second wife."

"Is there no record?"

"None that I know of. I've told you all that is known about the Vanes. I could tell you a thousand tales that circulate among the ignorant hill-billies around here. One is that Randall Vane sold his niggers, got his pay in gold, and hid it somewhere about the old Vane House. Ad March says Cap'n Franklin Vane paid him a twenty-dollar gold piece about a year ago that was minted in 1856 and looked like brand-new. I didn't see the coin."

"Why, judge, you don't suppose there is anybody silly enough to believe a buried treasure story, do you?"

"Son, there's people along this river and back in the hills that's ignorant enough to believe anythin'. Adam March got to be postmaster at Vaneburg because he could read."

"I see," said Price Stanley, who was doing a little thinking about the Vane murder on his own account. "Who would inherit Vane's Mill and the land if it could be proved that Myra Vane was not the granddaughter of the captain?"

"Why—why, nobody. Old Anson Vane had one daughter. She married a hill-billy, and he disowned her. He left everything by will to Randall Vane, and it passed on down to Cap'n Franklin Vane."

"That leaves out Captain Vane's aunt, I see," agreed Price.

"But still, this property descended from, the original Anson Vane, and can only be inherited by his descendants. If the line to which he willed it is broken, it would go to other descendants of his body, whether he intended it should or not."

"Oh, it would?" said the judge. "Do you know anything about law?"

"I may know a little about it," smiled Price Stanley. "The dean of the law school of the State university thought I knew enough at the end of four years' study to give me a diploma and see me admitted to the bar; but I never practiced law. I'm a born stock-man."

"Huh. Well, I may need a lawyer before this mess is over. Come on. We better get back to your camp before them wild drovers of yours come over here to take you out of jail."

THEY GOT INTO the old buggy and trundled back across the bridge. At the camp Price told Dave Baker he was going on to the Vane House to sit up with the dead, while the doctor got some sleep.

They found the old doctor nodding in the library, while Captain Vane slept the last sleep in an adjoining room. A few minutes later Mrs. Vane came in.

"I came back with the judge," explained Price, "to divide time with him and the doctor in keeping watch."

"That was kind of you," said the lady. "Don't go, doctor. I'll feel better if you are in the house. Myra is resting now, but it was a terrible shock to her. You and Judge Short can lie down in a room just across the hall. I'll show you."

"Call me if you want me, Price," said Peg Short, as he passed Stanley's chair.

The next minute Price Stanley was alone in the great

library, with an open door between him and the dead master of the house.

Price was not afraid; he just felt creepy. He had sat up with the dead, but never alone before. The custom in his country was for two or three to sit together.

Price settled himself in one of the great leather-covered chairs and looked about him. The room was well lighted by a large lamp. He had heard of such places, but had never been in one before. Banks Stanley had a good home, but he was middle-class. His tastes were utilitarian. All he asked was comfort and convenience. Here was richness without ostentation. The home of Randall Vane about as he had left it.

On the marble mantel were branching silver candlesticks and small pieces of rare statuary. The deep-piled carpet was clearly Persian. The bookshelves that ran around the room were low, and above them hung portraits of different periods. That tight-lipped old fellow, with the piercing eyes and bushy brows, might be, in fact was, old Anson Vane, who had disowned his daughter for marrying beneath her station.

Price sat for an hour just looking about the room and wondering what the rest of the house was like. The library was at the back side of the house, and a deep bow-window looked out on the terraced back yard and the old gray mill.

Old Anson Vane had looked out that window and watched the workmen lay the stone of the mill. Shrewd Randall Vane had looked through it at the mill in its prosperous days. Captain Franklin Vane had looked out on the faded glory of the Vanes and dreamed of what the mill and

Vaneburg would have been like if the Confederacy had not been lost and his soul killed.

The room seemed close. Price Stanley crossed noiselessly to the window and raised a sash. He glanced out across the back yard and on to the old mill, now softened by the light of a full moon. He turned and sat down near the window. Then he caught his breath.

Opposite him, over one of the bookshelves, was a life-size portrait of a smooth-faced boy. The golden hair, worn rather long, curled slightly at the ends. There was laughter in the blue eyes and a winning smile on the rosy lips. Every feature of the sensitive face was perfect.

Not merely a handsome boy, but beautiful in face and figure. A mother must have had that picture painted in order to keep her lovely boy after he became a man, Price told himself. If Myra Vane was Benton Vane's daughter, then that picture was Benton Vane in his boyhood.

The picture was beautiful, yet there was something sad about it. He turned away and looked out the window again. Strange, eerie thoughts were in Price Stanley's mind as he stared out across the yard and on beyond to where he and Myra Vane had found her grandfather's body.

A chill passed over him as he heard a soft, rustling sound. He turned his head and stared. For a moment he thought the boy in the picture had put on some kind of soft, clinging white garment, stepped out of the frame, and stood looking at him. It was Myra Vane.

3

A BROKEN SILENCE

"I BEG YOUR pardon, Mr. Stanley," said Myra Vane, as Price finally got enough control of himself to rise. "I—didn't mean to startle you. Grandmother has gone to sleep. I could not sleep, and anyway I—I—"

She stopped as if she could not say the next word.

"Take a seat, Miss Vane," said Stanley, now in full command of himself. "I shall be glad to have your company."

Myra sat down in another chair near the window, and when Stanley was seated she went on.

"I was going to say that I wanted to talk to you, because you are from the world out yonder. I have seen it. In my school days I went back and forth on the stage. I saw the tall blue-stem grass in the prairie country. I saw farmhouses, schoolhouses with happy children playing and shouting about them.

"Four years ago, at seventeen, I finished school and came home. Since then I have been in this old house."

Price wondered for a moment if her grandfather's death had upset the girl's mind. He said nothing and a moment later she went on more calmly.

"Mr. Stanley, I'm distraught. Perhaps I shouldn't say such things to a stranger, but I think I shall really go mad,

unless I can see some way out. Some ray of hope. I—have
stayed here because there was no place for me to go and
because grandfather was here. He was my only relative on
earth. Grandmother is—not really my grandmother. Of
course, I knew grandfather was feeble and infirm, and that
he must go some day, but not—in that horrible manner."
She stopped and shuddered.

"Don't think of it like that," said Price, gently, wondering
what her reaction would be if she knew that her grandfather had been murdered.

"I—can't help thinking of it, and of what will become
of me after—he is put away. I— Mr. Stanley, you can't
understand. I—don't even know who I am. Grandmother
told me the strangest things to-night. They—never saw
my mother. They don't know that my—father was even
married."

"I understand, Miss Vane, but—there is your father. You
are a granddaughter of Captain Vane, if that is Benton
Vane's picture."

"It is Benton Vane's picture," she said, "but grandmother
has told me terrible things about him. She says he was—"

Crash! Bang! Two shots tore the night, out in that
terraced back yard. A pane of glass in the window shat-
tered and tinkled to the window sill. Price Stanley sprang
to his feet, caught the girl up bodily, and carried her into
the hall out of harm's way. Then releasing her, he dashed
down the stairway that led from the hall to the back yard.
As he stepped out the open door, he saw a man lying on the
ground in the middle of the yard and another just passing
out the back gate.

Price jerked his two derringers from his pockets, and

fired at the fleeing man. In his excitement, he forgot that there was no accuracy with those stubby guns, beyond ten feet. There was no telling where his bullets had gone, but the man he had shot at sped across the mill yard and disappeared beyond the mill.

PRICE WALKED TO where the man lay on the ground. Then he was stopped, horror-stricken. The dead man was Malvin Tebo! He was still staring at the still form when he heard Peg Short's wooden leg tapping the steps, then coming on across the yard. Price didn't really rouse from his stupor of surprise until Peg Short said, quietly, at his very ear:

"Why did you kill him?"

Price didn't answer at once, and Peg Short spoke again.

"Tell me quick, so I can figger how to get you out of it. Malvin Tebo was a big man in this settlement. He comes from Rolling Fork, and the people over there will be riled about it."

"I didn't kill him," said Price. "Some shots were fired out here, and I ran out to see what had happened. I found him lying right here."

"But you've been shooting," persisted Peg Short. "You've still got yo' guns in yo' hands."

The moonlight was glinting on the Golden Derringers, which Price Stanley held in his hands.

"Yes, I fired twice at a man who ran out the back gate."

Dr. Potts came wheezing across the yard.

"H'm! What is it, Peg? What's the trouble now?"

" 'Nother body for you to examine," grunted Peg. "Law allows you three dollars for passin' on cases. If this keeps up, you'll bankrupt the county."

They wondered if that
bullet hole marked
a mistaken target

"H'm, h'm, h'm! Square through the head. Big enough to throw your hat through. Don't need a coroner to tell what happened to him. What was he doing here in the back yard?"

"Damned if I know, doc. I told him to go home and go to bed. I don't understand it."

"Did you mistake him for a burglar and plug him, Mr. Stanley?"

"No," replied Price, who had coolly ejected the empty shells from the Golden Derringers, replaced them with fresh cartridges, and dropped them into his pockets. "I had nothing to do with it. I heard some shots and ran out to see—"

"H'm! Better not talk too much. When I find a man dead on the ground, and another one standing over him with a gun in each hand, it always looks to me like the one with the guns might have had something to do with it."

"I tell you, I didn't—"

"What's—what's the trouble out here?"

Price turned quickly and saw Myra Vane, standing within a few feet of him, her white dress looking like snow in the moonlight.

"Miss Vane!" he gasped. "For the love of heaven, get back in the house. You're a perfect target in that white dress."

"Target?" she queried in a puzzled tone. "I a target? For what? I—"

Wham! There was no mistaking the voice of that gun. It was a rifle, and had been fired from the shadows of the old mill. The bullet struck one of the stone posts at the back yard gate, glanced off, and whined on over the house. For the second time that night Price Stanley caught Myra bodily up in his arms, and sped through the door with her.

"GO UP INTO the hall and keep away from the windows," Price said, as he set the frightened girl down inside the door at the foot of the stair.

Myra fled up the stair, while Price turned to face Peg Short and the doctor, who followed him inside for safety.

"Well," he said coolly, "do you still think I shot that crazy constable?"

"You may have shot him," wheezed the doctor, "but I am of the confirmed opinion that there is some one else out there with a gun."

"What are we going to do?" asked Peg Short. "We can't leave Malvin lie out there."

"I can," said Potts. "A man with a hole like that through his head don't need my services."

"I'll bring him in," said Price. "That last shot seems to have been fired from the upper story of the old mill, and it was fired at that white dress, but God directed the bullet. The other shot missed her by—"

"What is the disturbance, gentlemen?" asked Matilda Vane, as she reached the bottom of the stair.

Peg Short told her as much as he knew of what had happened.

"Strange," she said, calmly. "I suppose some of these terrible hill people have believed the wild stories of Randall Vane's riches being in this old house. They didn't dare come here while Captain Vane was alive, but now— It seems to me that they heard of his death quickly. How did the constable happen to be in the yard? I didn't ask for any one to guard the house."

"I don't understand it, Mrs. Vane," said Peg Short. "I told Malvin to go home and go to bed, but he's out there and he's dead. Can we bring him into the house?"

"No," replied the lady, bluntly. "He was not invited here. He came of his own accord, and got killed for his pains. There's an old servants' cabin out there by the big walnut tree. It is clean, and there's a bed in it. You can take him in there if you wish. Then, in the morning you can take him down the back way and on to Vaneburg by the old Mill Road. I don't want him carried through the house. I hope there will be no more disturbance to-night—or rather, this morning. It is almost daylight."

She turned and went back up the stair. Price Stanley noticed that she wore a dark dress. Perhaps it was to distinguish her from Myra, if she approached a window in this strange house. Perhaps, again, it was only because she was an old woman.

They found a candle and made a light in the servants' cabin. It was a stone building in good condition. There was nothing strange about it. There was one like it near every old Southern home. It was where the "house niggers" had lived in slavery days.

They carried Mal Tebo in and laid him on the bed. His "revolver" as he called it, was an old cap-and-ball Navy. It had not been fired.

THEY CLOSED THE door and went back to the house. Stanley shaded the lamp, so there was little light in the room, and the three sat down in a close group, well away from the window. The two chairs were still standing where Price and Myra had left them when the first shots were fired.

"What's that glass doing on the floor over there?" asked Peg Short, pulling at his long white beard in perplexity.

"The bullet that broke that glass was intended for Miss Myra Vane," replied Price. "It missed her but an inch or two, and— Good God! Look!"

He was staring at the portrait of Benton Vane. Instinctively, as he told of the shot, he had glanced across the room to see where the bullet went. There was a round hole at the meet of the brows in Benton Vane's portrait. Price wondered whether that bullet hole was an accident, or the killer had mistaken that lifelike picture for the girl herself, there in the lamplit room. Where had the man been who had fired that shot across the second story room? Out by the servants' house, perhaps.

"The whole damned thing stumps me," said Peg Short. "We knew somebody shot Cap'n Vane. Now, we know somebody tried to kill the girl. Looks like it's a drive to clean up the last of the Vanes, but— Funny thing that they didn't try to get Mrs. Vane. Damn funny. Funny how cool she takes it all, too."

"Oh, some people are like that," said Price. "They think it's an indication of poor breeding to get excited, or give way to their emotions. If it's a move to clean up the Vanes, she would be in no particular danger. The only reason any one could have for killing the Vanes would be to get hold of the property. She wouldn't inherit—"

"Why wouldn't she?"

"I was going to say she would inherit only a life interest. I understand she has no children to inherit."

"Huh! I ain't no law shark," declared Peg, "but I can see the horns on a dilemma. Most generally, they have two. This one has got three. Two of'em are a mile long. The other one is short and ugly. One of the long ones, and the most reasonable one, is this: Bent Vane was a rotten heller, for all his pretty looks. That picture is the spittin' image of him when he was a boy. He's around fifty now, if he's still livin', which ain't likely. The world wouldn't put up with him that long. He could have talked when he was drunk or something, and let some of them Western bad ones know too much. This gun stuff looks like them kind. Bent wouldn't kill his daddy, I reckon, if the reckless devil is alive, and he wouldn't kill his daughter—if she is his daughter! But I wouldn't put anything else past him."

"All right," said Price, "that's one long horn."

"Yes, and here's the other one. There might be some

descendants of Caroline Vane and the hill-billy she married, somewhere in these hills, that are doing this. You recollect Caroline, the old cap'n's aunt? But it would more likely be knives and clubs with them, than guns. That's all of that. It's a short story, but a long horn."

"Now about the short, ugly one," said Price.

Old Peg Short got up, stumped across to the door, peered out into the hall, listened a moment, came back, and sat down. Then he spoke in a low whisper:

"This may be treason," he said, "but—that cold-blooded old woman may be handling the whole thing. To my knowin' she ain't been out of this old house a dozen times in twenty year. Anybody would go crazy to live like that. She takes the thing too calm. It ain't natural. I ain't seen a tear in her eyes. Why didn't she hear the shot that killed Cap'n Vane?"

Peg stopped and not even the old captain on his bier was more silent than they. Dr. Potts had listened, but he had not spoken once while Peg Short was stating the case. At last, Short again broke the silence.

"There's your horns, and they don't none of 'em look purty, but the short one is the ugly one."

"Yes," said Price Stanley, "and they all probably miss it a mile. I'm glad they don't concern me."

"What do you mean, 'don't concern you?'" asked Peg Short.

"I mean it is daylight now. I'm going to pay my pasturage, turn those thousand cattle out, and hit the trail for my own open prairie country, where I can get a breath of clean air and keep a whole skin. Clear away from this lost and God-forgotten section of the world."

"I thought you was old Banks Stanley's son, but—"

"I am."

"You don't act natural and true to the breed, or you wouldn't get into a mess like this, then jump it. He—"

"Just a minute," said Price. "If you know Banks Stanley like you say you do, you know what cattle mean to him. He's got fifteen thousand dollars tied up in those cattle, and he wants that money in his pasture where he can watch it grow. I'm responsible to him for those cattle and I've got to drive them."

PRICE ROSE, AND stepped out into the wide hall that ran through the house from front to back. It was quite daylight now, and a dim light filtered into the hall through the fanlight over the front door, and the mullioned lights at each side of it. He met Mrs. Vane, who looked like a gray ghost in the dim light.

"I must be moving my cattle, Mrs. Vane," he said. "There are a thousand of them, and the usual charge for pasturage over night is three cents a head. That would be thirty dollars." He handed her two gold pieces, a twenty and a ten. She took them in silence. "Is—is that all right?" he asked.

"I'm sure it is. You would know. I know nothing of such things, but— Mr. Stanley, may I talk to you a few moments?"

"Certainly, ma'am."

She led the way through the hall and opened the door to a room that was opposite the great parlor in which Captain Vane lay. Price was thinking as he followed her that he was certainly popular with the ladies of that strange house. In the night Myra had sought him, only to have her story interrupted by an attempt on her life. Now the grand-mother sought an interview. How would it end? Perhaps—

He broke off his musing to look down at his boots, which were none too clean, and the soiled corduroys stuffed into the tops of them. The carpet in that room was white! Rich-ness and artistic beauty were everywhere. Price hesitated when she invited him to take a seat. He was afraid to trust his weight on those slender-legged chairs, but they were quite safe, as he soon found out.

"I know you think this is a strange house, Mr. Stanley, and it is. There is probably not another like it in the State, or in the world for that matter. I hope not, anyway. In order for you to understand, I must talk a little about myself, so you will understand why any supposedly sane woman is in such a place.

"I met Captain Vane early in the war. My people were violently Southern. He came to our house with some other officers. He was a widower a dozen years older than I, but a dashingly handsome man, brilliant and polished. I—I think I fell in love with the gold braid and panoply of it all. When a month had passed we were married. Within another month he was brought back to me, wounded. I nursed him back to the only health he has known since.

"Then when the war was over we came here. Long before then I knew that I had never loved him, and from day to day I grew colder. But in those days marriage was for life, for better or for worse. We found this house just as the rich Randall Vane had left it. An old Negro and his wife, whom Randall Vane had freed, had kept the house and cared for Benton, Captain Vane's son by his first wife.

"I soon learned that the house must be kept just as it was.

Captain Vane was a poet and a dreamer, but beneath that velvet surface was the iron that drove old Anson Vane to try to build a mansion and an old-world city in a wilderness. The old Negroes died, and Benton Vane went away. I was a slave, but I could stand it better after that terrible—

"Two years later, Myra was brought to us strangely. A woman brought her. She talked to Captain Vane, but I don't know what she told him. She didn't speak to me. He spoke only once. When he gave me the child, he said: 'This is Benton's daughter. Raise her as a Vane should be raised.'

"Mr. Stanley, I tried. As God is my helper, I tried. Myra has never loved me. She couldn't love me, because"—her voice sank almost to a whisper—" my very soul was dead. Franklin Vane's soul died when the Southern cause was lost. Then he made a slave of me, and my own soul died.

"I know you have wondered that I have shown no grief. I couldn't. I felt no grief. I—I'm afraid I hated him. I never dared to tell Myra anything about her father until—until he was gone. Last night, when I knew I was free from his bondage, I told her all I knew. I hated Benton Vane as a viper.

"I gloried in seeing his daughter suffer. She is his daughter. I know she is. He may never have been married, but Myra is his daughter. She is his image."

The woman was shaking with a terrible emotion now. Price Stanley, looking at her in wonder, pitied her sincerely.

"Don't—don't look at me like that, please. I—I want to do right. I want you to help me. I haven't a friend on earth, except Dr. Potts and that old shoemaker they call Judge Peg. The other people in the settlement hate me, because I hated them. They are clayeaters, white trash,

ignorant boors. Don't—please don't go away. I know you
are a gentleman. Dr. Potts and Peg Short are good men,
but they are old and helpless. They don't know what to do
in all this trouble, and I—can't even think."

"MRS. VANE," SAID Price Stanley, "do you know who is
doing all this shooting? Do you know who killed Malvin
Tebo? Do you know who tried to kill Myra Vane last
night?"

"No. I knew Tebo was dead, but have no idea who killed
him. I don't even know what you mean by saying some one
tried to kill Myra. She was in her room all the time."

Price sheered off that tack. Perhaps the girl didn't want
her grandmother to know she had talked to him. He set
himself for another question that should bring him some
knowledge of the tragic events in and around the old Vane
House. He approached it with dread, but it seemed time
to ask it. Mrs. Vane had asked him to help her. The answer
to that question would determine his actions.

"Mrs. Vane, will you answer one question, frankly and
without reservation or evasion?"

He was looking at her now, and she read coming tragedy in his dark eyes.

"Yes," she almost whispered. "So help me God, I'll tell
you if I can."

"Did you know that Captain Vane was murdered? Shot
through the heart before he fell into that pool?"

"No, no, no! Ah, God, not that! I didn't know! I don't
believe—"

"I can show you the bullet hole. Why didn't you report
that you heard a shot yesterday afternoon?"

"I didn't hear it. I tell you I did not. I—I must have been asleep."

"I should think a shot that close to the house would have awakened you."

"You—you don't believe— God pity me now! I'm—lost!"

Matilda Vane slipped from her chair to the floor and lay quite still. It was hard to distinguish her white hair and her pale face from the velvet pile of the carpet. Price Stanley rose and left the room. Returning to the library door, he said:

"Dr. Potts, Mrs. Vane needs you."

The doctor came into the hall. Price pointed to the open door, then went into the library and sat down.

"So you're not goin' yet a while?" said Peg Short.

"No," replied Stanley. "Will you let me see that bullet that Dr. Potts gave you?"

"Certainly. Here it is."

Peg Short handed over the bullet. It was but little mashed, and on the butt of it that fitted into the cartridge were the figures .38.

"Huh. Cartridge from .38 rifle," said Price. "Do you recall the direction of the wind yesterday afternoon?"

"Straight out of the north and pretty hard," replied Peg Short. "Why?"

"Nothing. I was just wondering."

"Are you goin' to stay and help straighten out this mess?"

"I'm going to stay and help bury Captain Vane. After that—"

"Mrs. Vane is all right now," said Dr. Potts, entering the library. "She wants to see you, Mr. Stanley."

VERY RELUCTANTLY PRICE went back to that beautiful room. Mrs. Vane lay on a couch. The day before that she had been still a beautiful woman. Now, as she lay there, her face was drawn and lined with age.

"Mr. Stanley," she faltered, "won't you, in spite of anything you may think or believe about me, take charge and give decent burial to a man who, in spite of all else, was an officer and a gentleman?"

"Yes, I'll do that."

"Thank you. And when it is done, will you please let me see you again? It will be the kindly act of a gentleman toward a woman in deep distress, if you will."

"Yes, I will come to see you afterward; but I must go now."

Price left the room, met Peg Short in the hall, and they went out the front door together. They talked a few moments, and then Peg Short said:

"Mighty fine of you to stay and help out with the mess, Price. Just what yo' daddy would do, and just what he'd want you to do. We'll get in doc's buggy. I'll drop you at your camp, then I'll arrange some way to get Malvin Tebo's body away from that place. Mrs. Vane talked about the old Mill Road. There hasn't been a wagon over it in twenty year. There's trees in it a foot through. We'll have to pack him out, if I can get men to do it. Funny idea that woman won't let us take him through the house and out to the Red Road."

"Yes," replied Price musingly. "Mrs. Vane seems to have a good many funny ideas."

"I'll tell you one thing," said Peg. "The killin' of Mal Tebo is goin' to start more hubbub than the passin' of Cap'n Vane.

Mal was a big man among these folks. They won't bury him here, though. He's from Rollin' Fork and they'll take him over there, where his folks are buried."

Half an hour later Price Stanley sat his Kentucky saddler at the west end of the old covered bridge and counted the thousand cattle from one side of the road, while Dave Baker counted them from the other.

"What did you make it, Dave?" asked Price.

"Even thousand."

"Right," said Price. "Take 'em and hit the trail. If I don't catch up with you to-night, I will some time."

"Now, see here, Price," said Dave, "I promised Old Man Banks that I would—"

"That 'll do!" snapped Price. "Take charge of the outfit and go on. That's what you are along for. To take charge when I can't."

Dave turned and trotted through the old covered bridge. Price watched until the cattle were through the town, then turned back toward the old Vane House.

4

TWO FUNERALS

DR. POTTS HUMMED about the old Vane House, calmly keeping such watch as was necessary. Mrs. Vane and Myra had given him breakfast, and he was quite content. Fretting and hurrying were unknown to him. He went out to the cabin in the yard, when Peg Short came up the steps from the mill yard with half a dozen men and a stretcher. Among the men was the scowling, speechless Ad March.

Price Stanley met them, helped get the body down the steps, then followed on around the mill and along the Mill Road, through the tangle of brush and briers that were so thick in places they had to cut a way through them. The other men, like Ad March, kept their tongues still. They were all hill people. Not a question was asked about how Malvin Tebo had met his death. They were not blind, and could see how it happened. They could guess who shot him, without showing it in their hard, brown faces. Every one of them was saying in his mind: "That damn' cattle drover, most likely, but it ain't my quarrel. Let the Rollin' Fork boys 'tend to it."

Price followed the strange *cortège* on to the place where the old Mill Road came up the hill at the west end of the bridge, old Peg stumping by his side. They stopped at the

end of the bridge, watched the pall-bearers as they clattered on across the loose flooring.

"Well, my part of that job's done," said Peg. "They'll get
a wagon and take him around to Rollin' Fork. I reckon
we'll hear plenty more from that buryin' without listenin'
now. I sent some hands to dig a grave for the cap'n, and a
wagon will bring the coffin out right away. It ain't much of
a coffin for a Vane, but it was the only one I could get that
was long enough. Ad March don't keep a very heavy stock.
He ain't prepared for a run in coffins like he's apt to have,
if this mess keeps spreadin'."

Price Stanley made no reply. They walked on around
the Red Road to the old Vane House, and Price saw the
men digging the grave. The Vanes, from old Anson and his
wife on down, had been buried in the family plot, out in
the woods just south of the house and a little way from the
road. Half a dozen men were working at the grave. They
were talking until Price and old Peg came in sight, then
they were as silent as the tombstones about them.

THE COFFIN CAME. Price, Peg Short, and the doctor put
the body in it. Myra Vane stole into the room, and took
one last look, then the lid was screwed down. By noon the
grave was done. There was no minister, no ceremony. Three
of the men left their hats on the portico, came in, and with
Price, Dr. Potts and Peg Short, they carried the casket out
and on to its last resting place. The two women, closely
veiled, followed and stopped a little way from the open
grave. The only sound, except that of clods falling hollowly
on the boards that covered the coffin, was one long, tearing
sob from Myra Vane.

So, unsung and unwept, but for that single sob, a warrior

was laid to his last long sleep. The grave was filled, and the two women walked back to the house with Dr. Potts.

"Decent burial for a man who, whatever else he may have been, was an officer and a gentleman," mused Price Stanley. "It wasn't a funeral fit for a dog. Even the men who filled his grave hated him. They would have stabbed his poor clay through the coffin with their picks, if they had dared."

Price and Peg Short walked back to the house together.

"Well, Price," said the old judge, "I'm afraid the planting that's bein' done to-day is goin' to raise a heavy crop of trouble for somebody,"

"Yes," replied Stanley, "It is quite likely that those who are planted are more fortunate than some they have left behind."

They met Dr. Potts in the front yard, and stopped under a tree.

"You two listen to me a moment," said Price. "I haven't stayed here because I want to stay. My duty was with that herd of cattle. I am staying because a woman who is in more trouble than she can even guess has asked me to stay."

"Aim to take a look at the horns of that dilemma?" asked Peg Short.

"I've got to do it."

"What do you think about the short, ugly one?"

"Nothing to it. A man did that shooting, and there's not a man on earth that Mrs. Vane could control. She has just lived here in prison until she's slightly off center."

"You're right there, Stanley," said Dr. Potts. "I've been that woman's doctor for a long time. She's not bad."

"I'm mighty glad to hear you two say that," said Peg

Short. "That short horn did look mighty ugly to me for a while. Now what are you goin' to do, Price?"

"We'll have to look at the other horns, but before we start I want to say this. Unless we watch very closely, somebody is going to kill one or both of those women."

"No!" said Dr. Potts. "Do you really think that?"

"I know it. Two shots were fired at the girl last night, with deliberate intent to kill her, and it's little short of a miracle that she escaped. I'm willing to stand my turn at watching the house, but I've got to get away if I make any investigation."

"All right," said the doctor. "I'll stay here the rest of the day, and you two look around. Then one or both of you can spend the night here, and I'll go home and get some sleep."

All three went into the house, and Price sought Mrs. Vane.

"I told you I would come back, Mrs. Vane," he said, "but just now I have but little to say. It is just this. You and Miss Myra are in danger all the time, night and day. Don't go out of the house when you can avoid it, and don't go near windows at the back of the house."

"Why, Mr, Stanley, do you really think—"

"Yes, I think the man that murdered Captain Vane intends to murder Miss Vane and possibly yourself. I am going to try to ferret this thing out, and if you will help, I believe I can do it."

"I'll—I'll do anything I can."

"Then tell Miss Vane, please."

"I will. She's in her room now."

WITH PEG SHORT, Price left the house, going out the back way and on to the mill. They stopped on the flat rock, where Captain Vane's pipe still lay, and dead angleworms from the overturned bait can lay drying in the sun. Price squatted down and peered through toward the river. There was but one tiny opening through which a shot could be fired at a man on that rock. Then the one firing the shot would have to be across the river, slightly downstream and two hundred yards away.

"I want to get on the other bank of the river," said Price.

"That ought to be easy enough. Old Cap'n Vane kept a boat. Come on, I'll show it to you."

They crept around the little pool and on through the thick brush and followed on to where the water from the old mill race found its way back into the river. Drawn up in the mouth of the tiny stream and tied to a tree, was an old rowboat. In it were two warped and twisted oars and an empty can for bailing the leaky boat.

"Well, by gum!" exclaimed Peg Short. "Thar's a woman's tracks. Looks to me you're wrong about that short horn not bein' ugly."

"That's not a woman's track," said Price, looking at the clear cut track in the soft ground. "That track was made by a man who wears about a number six boot."

"Number six," snorted Peg Short. "I've made boots all my life, and—"

"Yes, but you never made one like that. That track was made by the high-heeled boot that a Texas cowboy wears. I have seen those fellows a few times at Kansas City. They are beginning to drive cattle out of Texas, but they're all horns."

"Huh, I see now! The heel of that boot sticks forward and makes the track look short. Well, that settles it. That heller of a Bent Vane has talked and some of them Western bad men have come here to— Shorely Bent Vane wouldn't kill his own daddy and try to kill his daughter!"

"I don't think he would," said Price. "Come on. Let's cross the river."

"Well, that looks like it's the long horn after all," said Peg, as he took his place in the boat. "I'm glad it ain't the short one. I hate to think of a woman doin' a thing like that."

"A woman can do some pretty bad things, when she gets into the crime game," said Price, "but—"

"Hey, Price! This is dangerous, right out here in the open river. If them Texas toughs are in the brush with .38 rifles, like you said—"

"Not .38 rifles," smiled Price. "Just one .38 rifle. That would be enough, but I don't think the gentleman is here right now."

They crossed the river, tied the boat, and climbed the bank. Price located the spot from which he could see through that tiny opening, over the top of some low bushes, and on to Captain Vane's flat rock. He motioned Peg Short to him and pointed to some of those same tracks of a high-heeled boot on the ground. Then he stooped and picked up something. It was a .38 cartridge shell.

"I feel better," said Peg Short, as they tied the boat again in the mouth of the old mill's-tail. "I feel a little safer in this brush, and I feel a little more certain that Mrs. Vane ain't in on the killin'."

"I'm positive now that she knew nothing about the murder of Captain Vane. With the wind in the north and her in the house, she couldn't have heard the shot from that spot on the other side of the river. It is fully four hundred yards, and about forty-five degrees south from the house."

"What about them tracks on this side?"

"Made last night, when he came back to get the girl and Mrs. Vane, after he knew he had killed the captain. Come on. There's nothing more to see here."

They climbed into the mill yard, and went into the decaying old mill. Price climbed the rickety stair and looked about him. He approached a west window that looked levelly into the back yard of the Vane house. There on the floor, he picked up another .38 shell.

Price stood looking toward the house. It would be easy enough to shoot into the back windows of the house from that window; but the shot that had been fired at Myra, or at Benton Vane's picture, had not come from there. It was at the wrong angle. That shot could not have been fired from anywhere about the mill.

Clearly, that first shot that broke the window and struck the picture had been fired from the flat roof of the old cabin. Then the killer had seen Malvin Tebo in the yard and killed him to avoid discovery. He had met some difficulty in getting to the ground after firing the two shots, and was just going out the gate when Price reached the yard.

What Malvin Tebo was doing in that yard, no one would ever know. As good a guess as any was that he thought himself a bit of a sleuth. He suspected Price Stanley and went there to watch for him.

BACK DOWN THE stair Price went, and he and Short went on to the house. They found Dr. Potts on guard—he lay back in one of the big library chairs, sound asleep. Price made no comment. It could do no good. The old fellow had slept none the night before. He was corpulent and sluggish by nature, and had simply gone to sleep. Price had undertaken what seemed an impossible job, with very little help.

Mrs. Vane heard them talking and came in. Price asked to talk to her privately, and she took him to the great parlor, where Captain Vane's body had spent the night before. The room had been righted. The windows were open, and the south wind was swaying the heavy curtains. The same richness and beauty were here that he had seen elsewhere in the house. It was all a generation out of date, but rare beauty and elegance never grows old. It is the flashy things that fade.

"Mrs Vane," said Price, when they were seated, "I am ready to talk to you now. I had meant to ride on after my cattle, when the burying was over, but I can't do that now, without—" He hesitated.

"Without what?" she asked.

"Without leaving one woman in danger of death, and perhaps—"

"Do you still think I—" Mrs. Vane stopped. She couldn't bring herself to say the words.

"I know you had nothing to do with the murder of Captain Vane, and I'm sure you couldn't have heard the shot that killed him."

"Oh, thank God for that!" said Mrs. Vane, in a low, agitated tone. "Then you will—"

"If you wish it, I'll stay here, and try to help you out of this trouble. I think it will be over soon. Whoever is doing this has struck terribly hard, and must either follow it up at once or quit."

"Thank you," she said, quietly. "It is a great relief to me.

Just make yourself at home here, and we will do what you tell us to do."

"That is kind of you," replied Price, "but I can't find out much by staying in this house. I think there will be little danger until night. So I am going to look about a bit more."

Price and Peg Short left the house again. This time they went out the front way. At the gate, Price said:

"Peg, I'm not likely to need a horse in this mess. Vaneburg is as far as I am likely to have to go, and that is less than half a mile. I could put him in the clover field, but I want him to have grain and I don't want him stolen."

"I can take care of him for you," said Peg. "There's a stone stable, with a lock on the door, where I live, and I can get feed from Doc Potts."

"All right. We'll go to town now. I want to find out at the store who buys .38 rifle cartridges."

"You won't find out. There never was a cartridge in that store. Squirrel rifles and Navy revolvers is all the arms in this country."

"I'll take a look, anyway. You drive the doctor's buggy for us to come back in, and I'll ride my horse."

THEY CLATTERED THROUGH the old bridge and stopped in front of March's store.

"I'd like to get some cartridges," said Price, when he was inside.

"Huh? Get some what?" said Ad March, scowling at him across the littered counter.

"Brass cartridges for a pistol or rifle."

"Oh, them? I've heard of 'em, but I ain't never saw any. They use powder and lead and caps in this country."

Price didn't find out who bought .38 cartridges, but

he did find out that he didn't like the looks and tone of Mr. Adam March. He went out, mounted his horse, and followed Peg Short up Broad Street. Halfway up the slope, Peg stopped at the big stone stable. A little way from the stable stood two habitable rooms of what had once been a considerable house.

"Where I live," explained Short. "Father was a lawyer. All the family killed in the bombardment. I came back here after the war. Here ever since."

Price led the horse into the stable and unsaddled it. Peg Short locked the stable and showed Price where he kept the key. Then they got into the old buggy, and went up the hill to one of the dingy residences.

"Hasn't the doctor any family, either?" asked Price, when he saw no one about the place.

"No," snapped Peg. "What decent man would want to raise a family in a place like this?"

They helped themselves to grain and hay from the doctor's barn and went on back down the hill. After feeding Price's horse, they got in the buggy and went back to the Vane House. The only living soul they had seen was Adam March. He was standing in the door of his store, scowling as they passed on toward the bridge.

"Are you, Dr. Potts, and Adam March the only people left in Vaneburg?" asked Price.

"No. There are several families. One hill-billy and his wife live in Doc's nigger house and keep house for him. There's nobody in town now, though, but Ad March. He wouldn't be here, but he ain't allowed to close the post office until six o'clock. They're all gone over the hog-back to Rollin' Fork to attend Malvin Tebo's funeral."

Price glanced at his watch. It was just six o'clock. He looked back, as they turned onto the bridge and saw Ad March closing his store.

Night came on. Dr. Potts had rattled away in his old buggy, to spend the night at home. Price and Peg Short ate supper from silver plate on a mahogany table, lighted by candles in tall, silver candlesticks, and were waited on by Mrs. Vane and Myra. It was the formal service that the late Captain Vane had insisted upon, and the women had not yet realized that they were free from his domination.

Supper over, Price and old Peg repaired to the library. Peg Short drew from some place in his clothes two old Navy revolvers. They probably had not been fired a dozen times since the Battle of Wilson's Creek, but the caps on them were not cankered, and they looked quite business-like. Peg laid them on the table and said:

"Ain't likely to be any devilment until later, Price. I can make out awhile. You lie down on that couch and go to sleep."

Price was asleep in a moment. Old Peg Short sat in the unlighted room, watching for the moon to rise—and anything else that might happen.

5

THE MAD PREACHER

A VERY DIFFERENT affair was the other funeral. The wagon way to the Rolling Fork settlement led down the east side of Paramo River five miles to the confluence of the two streams, and then up Rolling Fork a like distance to the Rolling Fork meeting house and the heart of the settlement. The wagon that carried one of the mighty among the hillmen to his last rest went that way. The people of Vaneburg crossed the steep, flinty hog-back on foot by a trail that no vehicle could pass. It was only three miles from Vaneburg to the meeting house that way.

It was mid afternoon when old Parson Chaffin stood bareheaded by the open grave, a worn Bible in his hand. He was a tall, gaunt, grim-faced old man of powerful frame, who had once been a great fighter. He stood for a moment looking over the crowd, which was too great for the little meeting house.

They were plain hill people. The men wore cowhide boots, jeans pants, and hickory shirts. The younger women were clad in prints, while the older ones, for most part, wore the home-woven linsey.

Over to one side of the crowd, the parson fixed his eyes for a moment on a young man who was a bright spot in the drab picture. He was a remarkably handsome fellow of twenty-five, perhaps. Neither blond nor brunet, yet with a heavy, drooping sandy mustache and slate-blue eyes. It was not the man, but his raiment, that made the brightness. He wore a plum-colored woolen overshirt. At his neck a gaudy silk handkerchief was loosely knotted. His trousers were of pronounced stripe and stuffed into the tops of his boots, in the morocco tops of which were yellow stars and crescents.

At first the parson thought this young man was a stranger, and the sermon he meant to preach was not for strangers. Then he read the face and knew the boy was a Feeters. He didn't know which one, but he was Rolling Fork stock.

His eyes passed on to a group of women near the grave. One of them, a woman in her forties, perhaps, stood bolt upright, dry-eyed among the mourners. Her black hair, slightly shot with silver, was parted in the middle and combed over her ears. Her mouth was a grim line, with a snuff stick at one end of it.

The parson had not seen her for a long time, but there was no mistaking her. She was his cousin, Mahala Vane Chaffin, that was. He didn't know what her name might be now. Satisfied that no stranger to Rolling Fork was in that crowd, and unaware that the man who had shot Malvin Tebo was listening to him, the old parson looked out over the crowd and said:

"Vengeance is mine, saith the Lord, and I will repay." He waited a moment for effect, and then: "There is much misunderstanding of the scriptur'. The Lord says He will repay, but He don't say how. We know He won't come down here and smite the killer of Malvin Tebo with His fist or shoot him with a Navy or a squirrel gun. How is He goin' to square the killin' of Malvin?

"I'll tell you, my friends. We are all servants in the hands of the Lord. He is walkin' amongst us right now, though we can't hear His silent, stately steps. Before this getherin' breaks up, He is goin' to lay unseen hands on the head of the Rollin' Fork man who is goin' to be a servant in His hands and carry out His vengeance on the slayer of Malvin Tebo."

The parson stopped again to let his words sink in. Almost every man there was kin in some degree to Malvin Tebo, and four of his stalwart brothers stood together near the grave. The parson had heard of the young cattle drover, whom Malvin had sought to arrest, and he went on:

"A Philistine, a worshipper of Baal, has come out of the North. He has connived with the Philistine house of Vane, the haters and enemies of our people, and has shed the blood of the greatest man among us. But the Lord will raise up an avenger from among His people, even as He raised up Gideon."

The backwoods preacher was ignorant, but he was a natural orator. He knew his people, and he moved them with a terrible sway. For an hour he ranted. Part of the time he was extolling the virtues of the man who lay dead in the coffin, and of his family connection; but for most part, he was inciting the men of Rolling Fork to a terrible vengeance on the Philistine, the cattle drover who had come out of the North to do murder on a son of Rolling Fork.

There was no lack of mourning at that funeral. The wailing never ceased until the last shovelful of earth was on the grave and the crowd melted away. Old Parson Chaffin mounted his pony and trotted away up Rolling Fork, feeling that his oration had been a masterpiece. If his intention had been to incite the Tebos and their neighbors to murder and to get a lot of them needlessly killed, it had been a masterpiece, indeed.

HALF A MILE north of Rolling Fork meeting house, near a spring at the head of a draw, stood a tumbledown cabin. It was about a hundred yards from where the Vaneburg trail came down that side of the hog-back. Near the cabin stood an old, ramshackle wagon, while a little way from it two scrawny ponies grazed at the ends of the only two lariat ropes that had ever been seen on Rolling Fork.

Inside the cabin, Mahala Vane Chaffin busied herself cooking supper at the open fireplace. In spite of her rakish appearance, Mahala was of true Vane descent, for her mother had been a sister of the prosperous Randall Vane, which made Mahala first cousin to the late captain. The young man of the ornate boots and gaudy handkerchief sat on a box in the chimney corner, silently watching her.

"What's the matter with you, Cleech?" asked the woman. "You been moonin' around ever since we come from that buryin'."

"Mammy," said Cleech, "do you reckon that old preacher knowed what he was talking about, when he said the Lord was goin' to pick a feller out'n that crowd and sick him onto the man that kilt Mal Tebo?"

"*Naw!*" snarled the woman. "Lige Chaffin allers was crazy. He's got a power with these Rollin' Fork folks, though. If he'd been ketched young and teached somethin', he'd 'a' been a power anywhur."

"He can shore tell it, Mammy."

"Yes, if he'd jes' tell what he knows and stop. Hit wouldn't take him more'n a minute. Trouble is, he tells too much that he don't know. I didn't reelize how ignorant and behind times these Rollin' Fork folks is, until I come back here. The women looks like boogers, and the men ain't got no sense."

"Ain't like Texas, is it, Mammy?"

"No, hit ain't. I could make more money pickin' cotton one season in Texas than these Rollin' Fork women kin make pickin' geese their whole endurin' life. But I don't aim to pick ary one. I aim to have my rights."

"Mammy, when—"

"Never mind no questions now. I want you to tell me again about what that feller at Warlock told you."

"Why, Mammy, seems like I told you that enough. He said there was a yaller-haired heller around Warlock and Tascosa that was a plumb terror. Said he packed two guns, and when he didn't like the way a game was run he'd clean out a whole saloon and gamblin' house by hisself."

"That weren't all he said, were it?"

"About all, except that this feller got so scand'lous bad after a while that some cowboys ganged on him and shot him to shoe strings. Then they buried him on Boot Hill."

"Yes, and what did they say his name was?"

"I told you a hundred times, Mammy. They said his name was Warlock Bent when he was sober, but when he was drunk he called hisself Benton Vane, and put on airs."

"Yes, I'll bet he put on airs, drat him! Him bein' dead is the best news I ever heard in my life. I could listen to it all day. Come on. Supper's ready."

AFTER SUPPER THEY were crouched over the little fire in silence, when they heard heavy boots on the Vaneburg trail.

"That'll be Ad March, I reckon," said Mahala.

March came on and stopped at the open door.

"Come in, Adam," invited the woman. "'Pears like you haven't been very anxious to see yo' sister from Texas. I sant you word two days ago that I wanted to see you. Whyn't you come to the buryin'?"

"Couldn't get off," growled March. "Had to keep the post office open."

"Huh! Pay attention to me, and you won't need to keep no post office. This is Cleechie. You ain't saw him since he was a little boy. Cleech, this is yo' Uncle Ad March."

The two men shook hands awkwardly enough. Mahala turned the smoky lantern up a little, and the three sat down.

"Now tell me about that twenty-dollar gold piece you writ me about, clean down in Texas."

"Ain't nothin' more to tell than what I writ. Old Cap'n Vane paid me a twenty-dollar gold piece that was minted in 1856, and it weren't wore none."

"Huh! I reck'n not. Buried up in a chist ever since Randall Vane sold the family's niggers and buried the gold money he got. Now, listen to me, Ad. I aim to get my rights. I been in Texas ten year. Lark Feeters died up on me out there. I wouldn't give fo' bits for Rollin' Fork and everything that's on it. I'm back here for my rights, and when I get 'em I'm goin' back to Texas. Help me get my rights, and—"

"It wouldn't do me no good," growled March.

"Why wouldn't it? Yo're my brother, ain't you?"

"Step-brother," corrected March. "Thank God, they's nary drop of Vane blood in me."

The woman winced and sat silent for a moment, and then:

"I wisht they weren't none in me, but it's thar, and I can't help it. I aim to git paid for havin' it. I know you ain't my blood brother. My mammy, who was Caroline Vane and ten year younger than her brother Randall, married Lem Chaffin.

"I was the last one of her children. All the yuthers died up. Then my pappy, Lem Chaffin, died. When you and me was about four year old my mammy and yo' pappy, Tobe March, married. You and me played together when we was children. You help me get my rights, and I'll 'vide with you, like you was my blood brother."

"Huh! How you aimin' to get them rights?"

"I talked to a lawyer down in Texas. He said if all of Randall Vane's line was dead, and I could prove I was Anson Vane's granddaughter, they wouldn't be no question about me gettin' the property. Well, Franklin Vane is dead and Benton Vane is dead, and—"

"How do you know Bent's dead?" asked March.

"Ad, the Chaffins never would do nothin' for the rights of their women. When I married Lark Feeters I thought I was gettin' a man that would do somethin' about it, but I weren't. Lark taken me away to Texas to get clean away from the Vanes. But I brought Cleechie up different. I made a man of him. When he was sixteen I sent him on the trail of Bent Vane. He didn't find him, but he found where he'd been hellin' around, and found out he was dead. So, fin'ly, Cleechie and me comes on here to get our rights, and we're goin' to get 'em the only way they can be got."

"They's two women in the way yet," said March.

"Don't I know it! I spit like a mad cat ever' time I think about 'em. I could scratch they eyes out. I've saw that uppity wife of my Cousin Franklin's. She wouldn't spit on a Chaffin, and I don't reck'n she'd throw a dog's bone to a Feeters.

"She never brang Franklin no children, and she wouldn't inherit nothin'. I seen what they claim is Bent Vane's daughter, too. She's his'n, all right. The spittin' image of him, heller and all, when she was little."

"Well, how you aim to get around her?"

"Somebody got around Franklin Vane, didn't they?"

"No. He fell in the creek and drowned."

"Ad, you ain't much brighter than the rest of these Rollin' Fork folks, if you air postmaster over at Vaneburg. If that baby-faced imp of a Myry Vane will get on that rock at the right time, she'll fall in and drown, too."

"You mean—"

"Oh, you don't have to say it out loud. I aim to get my rights, and I know how to git 'em. I got to get 'em quick, too. Old Parson Chaffin riled these fool people terrible at Malvin Tebo's buryin' to-day, and they's no tellin' what they'll do. They may help, but I'm afraid they'll hinder. We got to work fast. I've told you the whole thing now. I don't ask nothin' of you but some watchin' and a good witness if we get into trouble. Point is, you just as well help us, because you are knowin' to what we have did and what we're goin' to do, and if we get caught you'll be pulled into it anyhow."

AD MARCH GLANCED toward the door like a trapped animal. He was trapped, and he knew it. He knew Mahala Feeters had some letters that he had written to her about

Randall's gold that would bind him up with her in any wild thing she undertook.

"See here, Mahaly," he said. "You can't see but one side of a house unless you go round it. You better look at the other side of this one. There's a cattle drover at Vane's that—"

"Great snakes, Ad!" cried the lady. "Do you think I'm plumb deef? I ain't heard nothin' else but how that cattle drover kilt Malvin Tebo, and all."

"I know, but listen. I reck'n that cattle drover has just plumb took up at the Vane House and that ain't all. He comes over to Vaneburg this afternoon and leaves his Kentucky saddler in Peg Short's stable and goes on back, like he aims to stay. He comes into the store and calls for .38 cartridges. Must pack a pistol."

"Listen, Uncle Ad," said Cleech. "Suppose he do pack a .38. That ain't no gun, and a Missouri drover ain't no booger. I've saw real cowboys at Warlock and Tascosa. They pack .45s. I've saw 'em work two guns. Saw 'em throw up a hat and put twelve holes in it before it hit the ground. Why, these drovers just think they're bad! One cowboy, with two guns, could whip all the drovers in Missouri. These fellers think they're cowhands. Drivin' cattle with whurps. They wouldn't know what a rope was fur, if they seen one. They still cluck to their horses and say, 'Giddap, Cholly.'"

"You haven't looked this one over yet," said March, who was not any too much impressed by the wise Cleech Feeters. "Mal Tebo told me himself that he tried to arrest this bird, and he knocked Mal cold with his fist."

"Well, what of it? Who wants to fight him with fists? We don't fight that way in Texas. A bullet would kill him just as dead as it would anybody."

"Shet up, Cleechie," said Mahala Feeters, "and let yore olders talk. Listen to me, Ad March. We can't do no more until that feller's out of the way. You can do that to-morrow easy. Then to-morrow night we'll finish this business."

"How can I get him out of the way?"

"That old fool, Lige Chaffin, fixed it for you to-day at the buryin'. When he got through rantin', every man on Rollin' Fork, cripples and any, thought the Lord had picked him to get that drover. All you got to do is pick yo' men and take 'em to Vaneburg, then let 'em pick a fuss with this drover.

"I'm told that Asa Tebo is goin' over there to run Mal's shop. Some of the women says Asa is a better man than what Mal were. If I was pickin' I'd let Asa run the shop, and I'd pick Sile Perkins for the Lord's anointed. One of the women told me that Silas never fit Malvin Tebo. She said the reason was that Sile was afraid if he ever hit Mal, he'd kill him. If you got him and Asa Tebo and one more hand, they can gang on that drover in a pinch, and that'll be all."

"That's a good idea, Mahaly. I'll go and see them fellers now."

"Fine. Cleechie will do the main work, but he'll stay right here until to-morrow night."

Ad March stole out into the night and took his way to Sile Perkins's cabin to inform that dangerous gentleman that he was the Lord's anointed to avenge the death of the man whom he had been afraid he would kill with his fist.

"Cleechie," said Mahala Feeters. "We're goin' to get our rights. Things are playin' right into our hands. Even Old Lige Chaffin is preachin' for us. The old fool! If Ad March pulls that fight, Sile Perkins will kill that drover the first time he hits him. Then if a fuss is made about it, Sile will tell that Ad put him up to it."

"It wouldn't break my heart none if Uncle Adam got his'n in the mess," said Cleech. "I don't see why we should split with him when I'm doin' all the dangerous work."

"There'll be plenty, Cleechie. No tellin' how much money Randall Vane buried up in that old house. I'm glad my troubles are goin' to be over. All her life my mammy worried because she couldn't get her rights. She et out'n tin plates and kept her salt and sugar in gourds, when she knowed her brother Randall was eatin' and drinkin' out'n silver. When mammy and Randall was gone, I'd been satisfied if my Cousin Franklin would just gimme a few thousand, but he treated me like the dirt under his feet. If his women had been human, they could slipped me a little and I'd been satisfied. No, they wouldn't throw Mahaly Feeters a dawg-bone. I know I'm bitter, Cleechie. I got a right to be bitter. I aim to take it all now. I've did without long enough."

Mahala fell silent, and she and her prided son sat staring into the embers of the dying fire, just waiting for the time to strike their last terrible blow at the House of Vane.

6

FISTS

THE MOST PERFECTLY opportune moments for carrying out plans, both good and evil, have a way of slipping by poor, fallible mortals. Of all the nights upon which to carry out the nefarious designs of Mahala Vane Chaffin against the remnant of the House of Vane, that would have been the perfect time.

Price Stanley had not closed his eyes for forty-eight hours. He had never ridden night herd, as cowmen do in the West. To lose sleep ruined him. He had not more than touched the couch until he was asleep.

He was awakened by some one strangling and making a terrible noise. He sprang up, plunged his hands into his pockets for the Golden Derringers, then stopped and looked foolish. The gray light of dawn was coming in at the bow-window. The person who was in the last throes of strangulation was old Peg Short, who was leaning back in the big leather chair, snorting horribly. Price shook him, and he sat up and stared about him wildly.

"I gannes, I must have went to sleep," he said sheepishly.

"Yes, I think you must have," snapped Price. "I thought you were going to wake me when you couldn't stand it any longer."

"I thought so, too, but how the blazes could I wake you when I was not awake myself?"

"No, you were not awake, and it's a wonder your throat is not cut. Go find out if those women are all right, and if you ever let any one know we went to sleep on watch I'll shoot you."

"Easy as she lays, son," grinned old Peg Short. "This ain't war time, and they don't shoot men for going to sleep on post any other time. I ain't goin' to tell it. I'm as ashamed of it as you are. If ary one of them women had yelled in the night, we'd both been awake quick enough. I hear the women rustlin' breakfast right now. So, no harm's been done, and we got a good night's sleep."

Price Stanley had no idea how much good that sleep was going to do him a little later in the day.

After breakfast Peg Short went out onto the front portico to smoke his old cob pipe and watch for Dr. Potts. The old jurist and cobbler had a good many things to think about as he smoked. He knew Captain Vane had been murdered, and Price Stanley had shown him where the man stood who fired the shot. He knew some one had shot into the house and some one had killed Malvin Tebo.

More than that, some one had taken a shot at somebody as they stood over Tebo's body in the yard. The whole thing was a bit hazy and involved to Peg. It could have been Price Stanley the man was shooting at, both times. He might have thought it was Price he was killing, when he killed Tebo. Anything might have happened.

Peg was no great hand at making deductions. This young fellow said he was Banks Stanley's son. That didn't have to be true. Men had lied, in time. Still, common men didn't

Snarling with anger, all three leaped on him

ride Kentucky saddlers and boss an outfit that was driving a thousand cattle over the Red Road. Price Stanley had wanted to go on with the cattle, and had said he was staying only because the lives of two women were in danger. Were they really in danger?

He and Price had slept soundly through the night. Peg chuckled inwardly at the thought. If the women had been disturbed, he had heard nothing of it. There probably would be no more rough stuff about the Vane House, but the men of Rolling Fork would never let the killing of Malvin Tebo pass unnoticed. Nobody knew who had killed Tebo, but everybody knew now that he was killed in the Vane back yard, and that the cattle drover was in the Vane House that night. He, himself, was not positive that Price had not shot Malvin Tebo through the head with one of the Golden Derringers.

Peg recalled the picture of Malvin on the ground, and Price standing over him with one of the murderous little

guns in each hand. Peg's pipe began to snore. He pushed
the tobacco down with his thumb, and went on smoking
and trying to puzzle things out.

MEANTIME, PRICE STANLEY had gone down to the old
mill to see if he could find any evidence that prowlers had
been about the place during the night. He found nothing.
He walked over and looked down at the flat rock by the
little pool. The two fish poles and the overturned bait can
were still there. The water seemed to have recovered from
the shock of Captain Vane's murder. It gurgled through the
broken mill wheel and sprang joyously into the little pool.

"Strange mess," mused Price. "I don't see anything more
that I can do. If that killer was coming back, last night
would have been his time. Guess I'll get my horse and go
on after my cattle."

Price returned to the house, meaning to tell Mrs. Vane
that the trouble was over and he would ride on after his
herd. There was something depressing about this old house.
He would feel better, with his Kentucky saddler under
him and sweeping on up the trail toward the broad prairies, with their blue-stem grass and pure clean air. These
thoughts were in his mind when he entered the door, but
when he reached the head of the stair, they fled. Myra Vane
was standing there in the hall, obviously waiting for him.

"Come in the library, please, Mr. Stanley. I want to talk
to you."

They entered the room and sat down.

"I was trying to tell you something the other night, when
those shots were fired. It was that I—must get away from
this house. It has always been a prison, with its ticking

silence, but now it's—it is—terrible. Grandmother acts so strange since—since grandfather is gone."

"In what way?"

"I can't explain it. She—seems frightened at every little thing. She told me not to leave the house and to keep away from the back windows. I don't understand—"

"You should. You knew some one shot into the house, and—"

"Yes, but I thought it was Malvin Tebo, shooting at you. I heard him tell Judge Short that you knocked him down with your fist and that is the worst thing one can do to these hill men."

"Listen, Miss Vane," said Price. "Malvin Tebo didn't shoot at any one. His gun had not been fired. Also, the shot through the window was at you, or at that picture, because the killer thought it was you." He pointed to the picture and she saw the bullet hole for the first time and gasped. "More than that, the shot fired when we were in the yard was intended for you, and if I had not roughly carried you into the house, for which I apologize, you would have been killed then."

"But why should any one want to kill me? I have wronged no one. I don't know these people."

"I can think of but one reason, and that is that you are in someone's way."

"I—I have always been in some one's way," faltered Myra. "I know I have been in grandmother's way, though I didn't know it until since—since— She has told me terrible things since grandfather is gone."

"Did she tell you that Captain Vane was murdered?

That there was a bullet through his heart when he fell into that pool?"

"No!" cried Myra. "Does she know it?"

"Yes. I, myself, told her. I told her to tell you, and for you and her to stay in the house and keep away from windows."

"Then you think some one means to kill the whole family? Was that why you stayed and let your cattle go on without you? Was it to protect grandmother?"

PRICE WAS LOOKING into her wide blue eyes now, and he read something there that would change his whole course in this tragic adventure.

"No," he said, and there was an odd, humming note in his voice. "I stayed to protect you." She read the message that flashed for a moment in his eyes and then he went on. "I am not going to leave here until this mystery is cleared up and you are safe, unless—"

"Unless what?" murmured Myra.

"Unless you tell me to go."

"I never will. It gives me hope to know that some one wants to protect me."

"I may not be able to protect you all the time. I may not be in the house. I may even be dead, when you need protection most. Can you aim and fire a pistol?"

"Yes, I was taught that at school, but—"

"Then take these."

Price drew the Golden Derringers from his pockets and presented them with the butts toward her. She started back, and her eyes went wide.

"Why—why—where did you get those?" she stammered.

"My father gave them to me," replied Price. "Is there anything strange about that?"

"No, but—" She walked to the massive table in the middle of the room, reached under the side, and pressed a spring. A narrow drawer shot out from the side of the table. In the drawer, lying on a folded piece of velvet and flashing the light from their embossed surfaces, were two Golden Derringers, exact counterparts of the ones Price held in his hands.

"No wonder you were surprised," said Price. "I had not supposed there was another pair exactly like mine on earth."

"Forgive me, if I thought for a moment that—"

"It was quite natural that you should think my derringers were those. They are exactly alike, in every way."

"Grandfather told me the story of them. There were only the two pairs made, by a famous gunsmith and artist in New Orleans. They were made for twin brothers, who had been inseparable from birth, looked alike, and dressed alike. They both became officers in the Confederate Army, were separated for the first time, and both died from wounds on the battlefield. One of them gave grandfather these two, when he was dying. I often wondered what became of the other pair."

"That's a strange coincidence," said Stanley, in a musing tone. "My father came by these two of mine in the same manner. He had carried a wounded major from the battle-field. The major died before he could get him to a field hospital. When the officer saw that he was going, he gave the derringers and his watch to father, started to tell him what to do with them, and fell back dead."

"Strange, indeed," said Myra. "It seems almost that these Golden Derringers have souls. That some tie binds them. I wonder if—"

Myra stopped, and bit her lip. She had almost said she wondered if those ornate weapons were a tie that would bind her and Stanley to each other.

"Yes, it is strange," said Stanley, "but strange things happen in this old world. I am glad you have them. Are they loaded?"

"Yes. Grandfather kept loaded arms in several secret places about the house. Only the last year he showed them to me, and told me I was not to tell grandmother of them, I helped him clean them and reload them sometimes. The last time I saw these, he said: 'Myra, I am going to give you these Golden Derringers and something else that goes with them on your twenty-first birthday.' That birthday is to-day, and it seems more than strange that this should happen."

"Just chance," said Price, "but the derringers are yours. Find a way to carry them on your person. Never try to shoot a distance with them, but if anybody touches you, put them against his body and fire."

"Touches me?" she said and shuddered at the thought. Then in a hoarse whisper: "Mr. Stanley, I know it is a terrible thing to say, but—do you think grandmother knows—knows anything about—"

"I don't know what to think. I only know that you're in danger and must watch every moment. I'm going to town when the doctor comes and see if I can learn anything. Hide those derringers about you and close that drawer."

Myra took the guns from the drawer and slipped them

into the pockets of a loose coat she wore. As the drawer clicked in place, Mrs. Vane appeared at the door.

"Judge Short said to tell you the doctor had come, Mr. Stanley."

WITH A PARTING glance at Myra, Price Stanley left the room and passed on out the front door. He and Peg Short met the doctor at the gate.

"H'm, h'm, h'm! How did the night pass at the seat of war? Any more killin's?"

"Not a one, doc," replied Peg Short. "Old place was quiet as a graveyard on Sunday."

"H'm, h'm! Can't say so much for town. More excitement than there's been since the Yankees shelled the place. The people came back from Rollin' Fork some time in the night. Dacy Plodgett and his wife were up early enough, if they ever went to bed, but they like to never got me any breakfast. Dacy told me some of my corn and hay was gone, and then him and Rilda Jane talked about Malvin Tebo's funeral. Said it was the biggest funeral ever held on Rollin' Fork."

"Yes," drawled Peg. "Rollin' Fork folks get noticed twice in their lives—when they're born and when they die. What do they say about who killed Malvin?"

"You know blamed well them hill-billies wouldn't talk to me about that, Peg."

"No, I reck'n not. Come on, Price. We'll go over there, and maybe they'll talk to us."

"Wait a minute," said Price. "It was quiet enough last night, doctor, but it won't do to get careless. Those women are in danger every moment."

"Well, I'll stay until you come back, and if anythin' happens, I'll do my best."

Price and Peg Short went on to town. As they went along, each was busy with his own thoughts. Price was saying to himself:

"So Captain Franklin Vane kept loaded guns in secret places about the house! Obviously, the old gentleman expected trouble. And this girl that I want to protect knows how to load and fire them. Looks like— No, she's helpless, and— Damn it, I never saw another woman like her! I'll never leave here until I know she's safe, and—something else."

ADAM MARCH WAS not in front of his store, but Malvin Tebo's shop was open, and three men stood in front of it. They were all easily six feet and as fine specimens of hill manhood as could be found. They stood in a close group and watched Peg Short and the drover turn into Broad Street and drive on to the old stable.

"Three contenders for the title," sneered Peg Short.

"What title?"

"Champeen of Rollin' Fork and Vaneburg. One of 'm is Sile Perkins, one is Asa Tebo, and the other is Candy Troboy. The pick of Rollin' Fork fists."

"And they've got to fight to see who wins the belt?" said Price. "I'd like to see the scrap. They're a husky lot."

"Yeah. They'll be damage done in that fight, whenever it comes."

There were probably twenty men in sight. Price was looking for a pair of high-heeled cowboy boots, but all he saw were the heavy cowhide boots of the hills. At the stable he found that his horse had cast a shoe.

"Huh!" he muttered. "I ought to have had those shoes reset a week ago. When I leave here I'm going to have to ride to catch up with my cattle. I'll just take my horse and have him shod now. Then we can loaf about town and listen while the job's being done.

"Good morning, gentlemen," said Price, as he led the beautiful horse to the front of the shop, where the three giants still stood in a close group. "I'd like to get my horse shod, and please use light road-plates. He—"

"Can't shoe him," growled Sile Perkins.

"Why? Haven't you any road-plates?"

"Yes, we got 'em. If we ain't, we can make 'em. We can make anythin' that kin be made out'n ar'n."

"Then why can't you shoe my horse?"

"Because, mister, we don't shoe horses for no damn' cattle drover. 'Sides that, yo' hawss can pack you a damn' sight furder than you'll ever get from Vaneburg without any shoes."

"What do you mean?" asked Price, stiffening in his tracks.

"I mean that you are the damn' cattle drover that got high-and-mighty with me over on the Red Road the other day. You was too good to fight a hill-billy then—or maybe you was afraid to fight like a man. Malvin Tebo couldn't take you, after you kilt Cap'n Vane, and you kilt Malvin, with yo' gun, but I'm goin' to take you right now."

Sile made a step toward Stanley and Price dropped his bridle reins. The horse turned away and trotted across the street, where Peg Short caught it. Price braced himself for the attack. Sile turned loose the blow that he had been afraid would kill Malvin Tebo. But, when it arrived, Price was not at home, and Sile's ham-like fist almost jerked his arm from the socket. Twice more the mighty Silas struck, with vengeance in his heart. Ad March had told him he was the Lord's anointed and he couldn't fail. Ad was standing in the door now to see that his prophecy was true.

THEN SOMETHING WENT terribly wrong with Sile's plans of speedy conquest. A hard left caught him on the jaw and shook him to his bullhide boots. He staggered, shook his head, and rushed in like a mad bull, head down and arms flailing.

Mr. Perkins was thoroughly angry, which was not good for what was the matter with him. He never landed on anything firmer than the air, while blows from some unknown source were raining on his face. In about a minute the spectators saw more blood than they had seen since last hog-killing. At last, when his eyes were almost closed and his nose and lips bleeding freely, Price socked him one right on the button and the mighty Silas lay down to rest.

"That don't say you're so damned good!" snarled Asa Tebo, as he sprang toward Price. "I'll take you, you dirty cattle drover and killer."

There was something about Asa that Price didn't like. The set of his nose, perhaps. He didn't help that nose any with his first blow, but he fixed it so nobody could ever make it beautiful or even comely. But Asa was a tough proposition. A smashed nose and a little blood meant nothing to him. He had suffered that often.

The next thing he caught was a hot one over the heart, that almost stopped it. Asa staggered a moment and came back for more. There was a crack like a pole-ax on a beef's head. The report came from somewhere in the neighborhood of the works that kept Asa's head fastened to his neck, but he didn't hear it at all.

As Asa Tebo lay down to help Silas with the resting, the count was two down, two out, and one to go. That one was going straight for Price Stanley in the form of Mr. Candy Troboy, pinch-hitter for heaven's anointed.

He was a wiry lad and much better on his feet than Sile and Asa. He couldn't hit anything, but he was making Price work himself to death, trying to kill him, for Price was really mad by this time. It came about the four hundredth dodge and landed in a place that would make wind scarce with Mr. Troboy for a month.

Price had reached for the solar plexus, but Candy wouldn't behave and he missed it. All he did was almost set Candy's shirt afire with the speed of the blow, and incidentally, take three ribs clean loose from the backbone, on the lower left side.

Candy kept his feet and reeled away, but he wasn't fit for fighting. Ad March, standing in the door of his store, saw what had happened. He didn't know it, but the three big louts, any of them stronger than Price Stanley, had jumped a man who had won plenty of bouts in the amateur ring. Price was about out of wind. He backed away and dropped his hands to his trousers pockets. Silas and Asa had got up and stood undecided as to their next move.

"Whyn't you take him, Sile?" called March from the store door.

"Go to hell!" snarled Sile. "You and old Parson Chaffin is both dirty liars."

"Gang on him, you fools!" roared March. "He's goin' fer his knife!"

The three giants had scorned help. Each of them had stood up and fought Price like a man. It was a disgrace on Rolling Fork to do otherwise. But now, at the snarling cry of a jackal who had not been in the fight, they turned beast. Battered as they were, the three of them swept over Price like a wave. The four went down in the dusty road, with Price Stanley at the bottom of the heap.

POOR OLD PEG SHORT stood holding Price's horse and helplessly looking on. He had his two old Navy revolvers on him, but he couldn't risk a shot at that mass of writhing bodies. He was quite as likely to hit Price as one of the others. Parson Chaffin's vengeance, it seemed, had overtaken Price Stanley after all, and he was being executed for a crime that he had not committed.

Boom! Boom! Two muffled roars. The Golden Derringers had decided that battle. Sile Perkins rolled one way and Asa Tebo the other, while Candy Troboy sprang clear and gained the blacksmith shop.

Price stood up, ejected the shells, reloaded the Golden Derringers, and dropped them into his pockets. Smoke was curling all about him, for the powder had set fire to the cotton shirts of both his victims. The onlookers sat stupefied with terror. Price was a raving madman now, with no thought of fear. He stalked to the store and confronted Adam March.

"You wanted somebody to gang on me, did you?" he roared, shaking his fist in March's face.

"Get out'n here, now!" whined Ad. "I'll have the law on you fer raisin' a disturbance in a post office!"

Price caught his arm, swung him to the curb, and kicked him into the street. Then he followed him.

"We are not in the post office now, damn you!" he snarled. "Come on!"

March turned and started to run. Price caught him and struck him a blow in the face that would have felled an ox, but the raging Stanley held him up and struck again, then dropped him in the dust like a rag. Turning to the terrified onlookers, he called:

"If any of you trash want any of this, come and get it!"

No one wanted any of the broth that Price Stanley was serving just then. Two of the men were putting out the fire in the garments of the dead men. The others were frozen in their tracks. Price took the bridle from Peg Short's trembling hand, and they turned away toward the old stable.

7

DEAD MEN'S POWER

NEITHER OF THEM spoke until the horse was inside, and then Peg said:

"Price, you may not want any advice from me, right now, but I'm goin' to give you some and you can take it or leave it."

"What is it?" asked Price.

"Mount that Kentucky horse and ride from here. Them Rollin' Fork folks are goin'—"

"Bah! They won't do anything. Look at the loafers, there on the street. They wouldn't take up the fight when I dared 'em to."

"Wait a minute," said Peg Short. "I'm not talkin' about these Vaneburg fellers. They're Rollin' Fork stock, but they're outcasts.

"Real Rollin' Fork people live in houses that have been in the family ever since the Osages and Delawares were run out of here. They'd scorn to work for anybody, or anywhere, except in their own fields. They think they're aristocrats."

"They ganged on me," defended Price. "I had to kill 'em, or get killed."

"Oh, I ain't blamin' you. If I hadn't been afraid I'd hit you, I'd have shot 'em myself, but that don't change the facts.

News of this will be all over the Rollin' Fork settlement by night, and they'll come prepared to get you next time."

"Listen, Peg," said Price, now more calm. "There are two reasons why I can't take your advice. One is that I never ran from anything in my life. I know I'm in the right, and all this stuff was pushed on me, and I refuse to run. The other reason is—" Price stopped.

"I don't see much use for ary other reason," drawled Peg Short, "but what is it?"

"A woman. I may be foolish, but I'll never leave here now until I find out who is trying to kill Myra Vane."

"How about Mrs. Vane?"

"I've thought of Mrs. Vane considerably myself," said Price, "but she doesn't seem to need protection very badly. So far as I know, no one has tried to kill her."

PEG SHORT TURNED his kindly blue eyes on Price and studied his face for a moment. Then he said:

"Price, I gave you some of the best advice I ever gave anybody in my life, and I know it, but—I'd have despised the very memory of you if you had taken it."

"Thank you a lot," said Price, "and now I'll tell you something. Your friend Adam March knows who is making the trouble at Vane House."

"What makes you think so?"

"I don't know. Instinct, maybe. He's the one that planned to have me beaten to death this morning. What did Silas Perkins mean when he said old Parson Chaffin was a liar? Who is Parson Chaffin?"

"Parson Chaffin? Why, he's a power among the Rollin' Fork folks, for one thing. The Chaffins are the oldest family over there. The old parson's granddaddy claimed that he knew Dan'l Boone. They're pretty smart folks, accordin' to their lights, but they're hill-billies, and old Anson Vane—" Peg broke off and stopped.

"Yes. What about Anson Vane?"

"Price, you're about to make me talk about somethin' that ain't often mentioned in Vaneburg." Peg Short sat down on the ground, leaned against the front of the stable, filled and lit his pipe. "It was Parson Chaffin's uncle that married Caroline Vane. Caroline had some children and they all died but one—Mahala. She also had a stepson, who was Ad March. I ain't heard of Mahala for years. She married Lark Feeters, and they went to Texas."

"While Ad March became postmaster at Vaneburg, because he could read and write," put in Price. "He learned from his stepmother all about the Vanes, hated them, and still wants the property. He's the one that told about that twenty-dollar gold piece that was minted in 1856, and— he's the dirty, sneaking, rotten thief that shot old Captain Vane, and told me he never saw a brass cartridge! He's the one who tried to kill Myra Vane, to get her out of the way!

"He's also the one that killed Malvin Tebo to keep from being caught. Then, on top of it all, Ad March charged me with killing Malvin Tebo and set those fellows on me, hoping to get me killed and cover his own tracks. Why—"

"Hold on, Price, you're goin' too fast and too far! You got me all out of wind. I've known Adam March all his life. He's a say-nothin' sort of feller, but he's got right good sense, considerin' the chance he had. Besides that, Ad March wouldn't take a chance like that for a billion dollars. He may know somethin', but he hasn't done anythin'."

"Probably not," said Price. "He very likely had his work

done for him, like he tried to do this morning. You'll see when this mess is cleared that Ad March and Parson Chaffin had a big hand in it."

"If it's ever cleared up," said Peg, musingly.

"It will be. I'm going to clear it up. I think w'd be doin' a Christian act to shoot Ad March like a dog, but let him alone. We can watch him. If he prowls about the Vane House while I'm there— Come on! Let's get back over there. No telling what may happen."

They drove back through town. The bodies had been taken away. The door of March's store was open, but not a soul was in sight.

NOTHING HAD HAPPENED at the old Vane House. Nothing was likely to happen there in the daytime. Dr. Potts was leaning on the gate when Price and Peg Short drove up.

"H'm, h'm, h'm! Glad you come. Lonesome as the devil here. Them two women stay hid up all the time, like chickens when there's a hawk about."

"I ain't been so lonesome over in town," said Peg Short.

"H'm, h'm, h'm! Thought I heard a couple of cannons over there. Yankees come back?"

"No, but there was some blood." Peg Short went on to tell what had happened. The doctor interrupted from time to time with a few "h'ms," but said no word until the tale was told. Then:

"Raise up that buggy cushion, Peg, and hand me them irons from under the seat. Looks like I might need 'em before long."

Peg raised the cushion, removed one of the loose boards from the seat box, and drew out a pair of long, slender revolvers, all loaded and freshly capped. The doctor took them and slipped them into his waistband.

"H'm, h'm! Brought 'em along. Didn't think I'd need 'em. Never can tell. Rollin' Fork folks ain't got any sense. Apt to go clean, rampin' crazy over this little fracas. Shot a squirrel out of the tallest tree in Paramo bottoms with these irons. Done it many a time. H'm, h'm, h'm! Let's go to the house. Nothing out here to stop lead but us. Don't like to stop it. Stopped some one time. H'm!"

They went on to the house. The two women may have been acting as if hawks were about all morning, but Myra seemed to think the hawks were gone when the three men entered the library. At any rate, she came out of her hiding-place. She went into the library, and a moment later she caught Price's eye, and nodded toward the open door leading to the parlor. They went into the big old parlor. A glance passed between the two old men which meant: "Let them go. We were young once. Youth doesn't last long."

IF THEY THOUGHT there was any lovers' meeting about that, they were mistaken.

"Mr. Stanley," said Myra, "grandmother has been acting stranger than ever this morning. She has gone over the house, slipping from one room to another, but trying to keep out of my sight. She seems to be hunting for something."

"That's odd. Would you mind giving me a plan of the house?"

"It is quite simple. On the south side of the main hall there are only this big parlor and the library. On the north side are two doors. One of them leads into a little *boudoir*, and beyond that is grandfather's and grandmother's room.

"The other door opens into a narrow corridor. Two bedrooms open onto this corridor, and there is also a second door into grandfather's and grandmother's room."

Price had sketched rapidly on a leaf of a tally-book which he carried in his pocket. He held out the plan he had drawn.

"That is an exact plan of the main floor," Myra went on. "Downstairs are the dining room and a big billiard room, which is under this parlor. It has been closed for years, except when grandfather would go in there on rainy days, or very cold weather, light the candles, and play billiards by himself for hours at a time. Unless the candles are lit, it is so dark that no one would want to go there. And of course the kitchen, pantry, storeroom, and a servants' room." She took the book and sketched in the rooms below.

"What is that you have left in the northwest corner of the basement?" Price asked.

"You notice everything, don't you?"

"I don't mean to be inquisitive," replied Price. "I am only trying to get a working plan of the house. I might need it."

"Yes, you might… I don't know what is in that corner. There is no door leading to it from the outside. Only solid stone walls. There is a door leading out of grandfather's room that I have never seen open. It is behind a heavy, tall dresser, and is always locked. I asked grandfather one time where that door led to. I never asked him again. No one ever asked him the same question twice, if he didn't answer it the first time."

"Thank you," said Price, putting the book into his pocket. "I just wanted to get the general plan of the house, so I could find my way about it in an emergency. No telling what may happen here before this trouble is over. I want to ask one thing of you, Miss Vane, and please remember, always, that I am trying to protect you. There are two windows in the east and one in the north of your room. Don't go near them, and don't go near any window when you can possibly avoid it. I am sure that another attempt on your life will be made, at any time."

"That is too terrible to think of, Mr. Stanley."

"Yes, it is terrible, but it is true. I have no arms except the two derringers I showed you. Do you think you could find me a pair of pistols?"

"Easily. Excuse me a moment."

SHE WALKED TO the door leading to the hall, looked out, then closed the door softly. When she returned she explained: "I wanted to know where grandmother was. I am sure she is in her room now, with the door locked. She is behaving strangely. Grandfather told me never to let her know where the hidden arms were. I don't know why, but he must have had a reason. Anyway—"

She stepped over to the broad fireplace, and motioned him to follow. They were now out of view of the two old men in the library, and Myra was leaning against the mantel at one side. "Take them quickly," she said.

Price didn't see anything that she had done, but a panel under the mantel shelf slid noiselessly aside, and two long, slim revolvers lay before him, in a little niche. They were silver-mounted and beautifully chased. Price didn't stop to admire them, but slid them into his waistband, out of sight. Myra moved, and the panel slid back in place again.

"This is a strange house," said Price. "It would be strange

in any country, but stranger still out here in these hills of the West."

"Yes, it is a strange house. Grandfather told me that the men who did the work were all dead long ago, and no one knew the secrets of the walls and furniture but himself. He said Anson Vane was a most peculiar man. He had traveled in the Old World in his youth, and had patterned these secret places after some he had seen in old castles over there. He was an expert worker in wood, himself, and made many of the queer things that are in the house. Grandfather showed me a few of them, but not all, I suppose. At any rate, he never showed me what was behind that locked door."

They went on talking, but their conversation was bordering on personal matters, and the things that Price would have liked to say to her, if the time had been opportune.

It was at dusk that evening, after an early supper, that Price said:

"I'm going to watch outside until after midnight. You probably would not sleep if you went to your room. Dr. Potts and Peg Short will sit in the library without a light. Won't you stay in the big parlor, at least until I come in?"

"I'll—do anything that you would ask me to do," Myra replied.

Price went away to his sentinel duty with a new reason for staying at the old Vane House until that mystery was cleared up. He took a position in the deep shadows of the back yard where he could see all of the back windows of the house, without being seen. By turning his head and peering through the fence he could see the mill and the mill yard. Ad March, whom Price was now sure had been doing the shooting, was pretty badly bunged up, and not likely to be out that night; but Peg had suggested that if Ad was in on the mischief he would get some one else to do the dangerous work. Anyway, it could do no harm to watch.

So began what was to prove another wild night at the old Vane House. Stillness was over the old place, and a great, peaceful calm, but that could and would pass.

MEN OF VANEBURG had put Asa Tebo and Silas Perkins in coffins and placed them in a little building at the back of March's store. That was as far as they would go. Not one of them dared cross the hog-back and carry the news of disaster to Rolling Fork. They knew that the first question asked would be why they had not got this Philistine, this wild drover who had killed three of the mightiest men that Rolling Fork had ever known. They knew that they had no answer that would satisfy the Chaffins, Tebos, Perkinses and Troboys. So they were calmly waiting to see what would happen.

Just at sunset two battered men plodded weakly along the trail that led from Vaneburg up the hill, over the hog-back, and on to Rolling Fork. They were Adam March and Candy Troboy. Every breath sent a knife stab through Candy, for the ends of some broken ribs were jabbing his left lung at every step. Ad March had a terrible headache, and his face was a ruin. It was growing dark when they reached the foot of the hog-back, and the Rolling Fork side.

"You go on down to the settlement, Candy," said Ad March, "and tell 'em what happened at Vaneburg. I'm just plumb tuckered out. I aim to stop at my sister's cabin."

"Yes, of course you aim to stop somewhere, damn your

sorry soul!" snarled Candy. "Come over here to Rollin' Fork and tell Sile Perkins that he's the anointed of the Lord, to chastise the Philistine what kilt Malvin Tebo. Tell Asa and me that we are to be there to drag off the carcass, after Sile knocks this Philistine gent to kingdom come.

"Then you sick the three of us on this he-tiger, and stand back and yell. You watch him kill Sile and Asa, and break everything in me that 'll even bend. Then, damn yo' sorry lights, you ain't got the spine to face Rollin' Fork and tell about it. Go on to yo' sister's and crawl under the bed, before I finish what that Philistine started and ruin you complete."

Candy stumbled on down the trail, muttering curses against Ad March and old Parson Chaffin. He would tell the news, and he would tell it plenty strong, if he lived to reach Bill Troboy's house, which he doubted.

8

THE WITCH OF ROLLING FORK

MAHALA FEETERS SAT in her cabin alone, munching a crust of corn bread by the light of a smoky lantern and musing over her bitter fortune. She would soon get her rights now, she told herself. Ever since childhood she had dreamed of the day when she would finger her share of old Randall Vane's gold, and would buy all the things her avaricious heart craved.

Hers had been a bitter life indeed. Her father had been too trifling to make a living for his family. As a matter of fact, his children had all died for want of proper nourishment, except Mahala, who had apparently been too tough for even that hard life to kill.

She had grown up to be a pretty girl, after Lem had died. Probably because her stepfather had been a little better rustler. The hard chin and straight, grim mouth of old Anson Vane had been there all the time, of course, but they had not become so noticeable until age and bitterness had developed them.

Mahala had been the belle of Rolling Fork, and could have taken her choice of the young men, but she had waited too long. There had been a reason for that waiting, and Mahala cursed horribly when she thought of it now.

Finally she had married the handsome but worthless Lark Feeters.

Instead of standing up for her rights, as she had hoped he would do, and compelling the Vanes to give her at least a part of Randall Vane's gold, half of which belonged to her, Lark trembled at the very thought of facing a Vane. Mahala nagged him unceasingly, and when Cleechie was about ten years old Lark took Mahala and the boy to Texas. He escaped the menace of the Vanes, but he had to die in order to escape Mahala's nagging.

Mahala stopped munching, and looked at the ends of her fingers. She imagined she could still see the hang-nails, the pricks and the scars from cotton bolls, when she and little Cleechie had slaved in the miasmic fields of the Brazos Bottoms, in Texas. Picking cotton. Slaving for a purpose, and saving like misers. Saving to get Cleechie an outfit by the time he was sixteen, so he could go away to the plains country and be a cowboy. To work from ranch to ranch, until he found that heller, Benton Vane, whom Mahala knew was somewhere in the great Lone Star State.

She lived again those eight bitter years while Cleechie was on his long quest. There were things about those years that she had been ashamed for even the calloused Cleech to know. Mahala munched a few more bites, then muttered to herself:

"That's all past, now. I'll get my rights. I'll eat out'n silver dishes, and wear silk a while, like I had always oughta done, if'n I had half my rights. What right did my old grand-daddy have to cut my mammy off without a dollar, because she married a Chaffin? He brang her up out here in the wilderness. Randall Vane, damn him, could go to the Land of Nod, or some place, and get him a woman of his own sort. Ca'line, bein' a girl, didn't 'mount to nothin'. She could do without ary man.

"If old Anson hadn't been a fool, he'd 'a' knowed she wouldn't do without one. She married Lem Chaffin, and I glory in her spunk. From all accounts, he were a right smart figger of a man. But old Anson kicked her out and forgot her!

"Well, if there is ary Vane left on earth when I get through, he won't fergit me! Talk about jestice. They ain't no jestice in this world. Them that gets, has. Them that don't get, when they has a chance, is a passel of fools. I got my chanst, and I aim to get—"

MAHALA STOPPED AND listened. Some one was coming.

"Huh! Cleechie must have worked fast. Don't look like he has hardly had time to— Hello, Ad! Have you finally come to life?"

"Just barely," groaned Adam, as he sat down on the other box. "Where's Cleech?"

"Cleechie went over to the Vane House this evening, to call on his cousin, Miss Myra Vane. She's a lovely girl. Her hair's like spun gold, she wears a silk dress, and a di'mant on her finger. Cleechie will do right well to get her." There was honey in Mahala's mocking voice, and fire in her eye.

"Cut out yo' nonsense!" growled March. "Where is the boy? I want to see him about something important."

"Ain't no nonsense about it. I told you where he's at. He went to the Vane House."

"Huh! He'd be a damn' sight better off if he had went to Texas, to hell, or any other place except the Vane House to-night."

"What you mean, Ad March?" Then noticing Ad's face, as he shifted it into the light of the lantern. "Good grief, Ad, what's the matter with your face? It looks like—"

"Never mind what my face looks like. Whyn't you wait until you heard from me, before you sent the boy over there? Whyn't you wait until that drover was out'n the way?"

"Ad March, I'm forty-six year old, and I ain't never done anythin' but wait, in all my borned days. I've waited for everythin' I ever got—and then didn't get it. I've waited on fools, and I've waited on cowards. I've waited for a man that had sense enough, and sand enough, to get my rights for me. I finally got one, but I had to born him, and bring him up myself, so's he would be a man. I brang Cleechie up to be a real he-man, and he'll get—"

"I've heard all that before," said March. "Listen to me." He went on to tell her what had happened at Vaneburg that morning.

"And you didn't send me no word?" she said, when he had finished the gruesome story.

"I couldn't send none, Mahala."

"Couldn't? What's the matter with them Vaneburg men? They're all kin of Rollin' Fork."

"I know, but they ain't Rollin' Fork stock in the true word. They're—"

"I know what they air, and I know what you air. If you had been any sort of a man you would have crawled over the hog-back to let me know, so's I wouldn't have sent Cleechie to the Vane House, and that turrible killer still there."

"I—I couldn't leave the post office until closin' time, Mahala."

"Shut up!" snapped Mahala. "If that big cattle drover had hit you about one more time, you would 'a' left the earth before closin' time. All we can do now, I reckon, is to wait until Cleechie comes in. I kin always tell what he'll do. I brang him up to be a man. That cattle drover might done what you said, but it don't sound reasonable. It don't matter if he did, he can't do Cleechie that-away. He's got more sense than to fight with his fists. He learned to fight in Texas, where they fights fights as is fights."

PRICE STANLEY HAD been sitting for two hours, watching tensely. He scanned the windows along the back of the house, and from time to time peered through the fence at the old mill and the mill yard. There had not been a movement or a sound.

He had just peered through the fence at the mill, lying drowsily in the moonlight, then glanced up at the windows of Myra's room. He knew Myra was not in her room, but there was a satisfaction in merely looking at her windows.

Then he gasped, as he saw the curtain at one of the windows move slowly aside. What could the girl mean? Instinctively, he glanced at that upper window of the old mill, which was fairly on a level, and in line with the window of Myra's room.

As he looked, there was a crash and a spurt of flame from the mill window. Price fired at the mill window, almost before the flame faded. The crash of his shot blended with a wild, agonized scream in Myra's room.

Price sped along the fence, jerked the gate open and reached the steps leading to the mill yard in time to see a man sprinting toward the steps leading to Captain Franklin Vane's fishing hole.

Price had the revolvers in his hands, and opened fire with them. At the second shot, the fleeing man fell. He sprang up and ran on toward the head of the steps. He was shooting to kill, and those long, slender pistols, loaded with powder and ball, carried like rifles. The man fell again at the top of the steps, and rolled down to the flat rock, where Captain Vane's fishing rods still lay.

The terrible screaming was still going on in the house. Price turned, bounded across the yard, and up the steps into the hall. His heart was pounding terribly. Not only with the exertion, but from the thought that he had found the woman he wanted in all the world, only to lose her at the hand of an assassin. He holstered the two empty guns, and clutched the Golden Derringers in his pockets. These would be better in the darkness.

At the head of the stair he ran into some one.

"Who— What is it?" came a puzzled voice.

Price's heart sang. It was Myra Vane's voice.

"Here! This way!" called Peg Short, appearing at the door leading to the narrow corridor, as he struck a match to light a candle which he held in his hand. "We've got to have a light. It's Mrs. Vane. Come on."

Price and Myra followed him to the back end of the corridor. The door into Myra's room stood open, and also the door at the end of the corridor, leading into Mrs. Vane's room. Peg started into Myra's room with the candle.

"Don't take that light in there," called Price. "Stay out here with it. We'll take Mrs. Vane into her own room."

For once in his life, Dr. Potts forgot to "h'm" before he spoke. He called from the dark room.

"I'll bring her. Hold the door open."

The screaming had given place now to a constant, whimpering, low moan. Mrs. Vane was laid on the bed in her own room. The candle was set on the mantel, and the curtains closely drawn. Dr. Potts kept up a steady h'm, h'm, h'mming as he examined the woman in the dim light. Her face was gray and drawn, as it lay on the white pillow. Once she spoke between her moans:

"I'm—I'm cold, doctor. So—so cold."

Those were her last words. Dr. Potts composed her on the bed, and closed her eyes. Then he caught up a white counterpane and spread it over the body. Myra made no outcry, but stood in wide-eyed terror.

"We can't do her any good," said the doctor. "That bullet passed near her heart. Let's get out of here and watch, or some of the rest of us will go the same way."

9

THE LAST VANE

PEG SHORT HELD the candle in his hand until the rest passed out of the death room into the corridor, then blew it out. Price took Myra's hand, to lead her through the corridor, then forgot to turn it loose. The moon gave enough light through the windows for them to see their way, after the candle had been out a moment.

Price and Myra went across the hall to the great parlor. Dr. Potts and Peg Short went back to the library, sitting down where a bullet from the window would not strike them.

"H'm, h'm, Peg, this looks bad. Only one more left. Seems like they mean to clean up the Vanes. Don't seem to want anybody else. Haven't tried to get us, but I don't want to get in the way of any bullets—they're blind. H'm!"

The old doctor had forgotten that the door was open, and Myra could hear what he said. She sat on a couch in the parlor by the side of Price, who still held her hand. She moved closer to him, shuddered, and whispered:

"I am the last of the Vanes. I'll be next."

"They shan't have you!" whispered Price fiercely, as he slipped his free arm around her shoulders. "Not until I'm dead."

There was a long silence after that, broken only by the ticking of two clocks, one in the hall and one in the library. They didn't tick together, and sounded like a lame man walking on pavement. Finally Myra spoke:

"I wonder what grandmother could have been doing in my room."

"We'll never know, I suppose," replied Price. "Didn't you say she seemed to be looking for something all day?"

"Yes, but what could she be looking for in my room?"

"I don't know, but I can guess. She may have been looking for the key to that locked door in her bedroom."

"Yes," said Myra thoughtfully. "Did you notice how she was dressed? She had on clothes that I never saw before. Clad for traveling."

"I noticed it. That was what made me think of the key. It takes money to travel. The thirty dollars I gave her for pasturage would not take her very far."

"I wonder—" Myra began, and stopped.

"We know one thing. She was killed by a bullet intended for your heart. I can never think ill of her, no matter what we may learn. We may never know, but—" Price stopped also. His thought was, "If I can have you, I'll never care." He did not say it, but merely tightened his arm around her a little.

The two old men in the library had quit talking. The two clocks limped on down the corridors of time. The two lovers sat in silence, wondering, wondering, wondering.

"LISTEN!" SAID MAHALA FEETERS. She and Ad March had been sitting for hours in the lonely old cabin, waiting for Cleech to return. "That's Cleechie, I reckon, but it don't walk like him."

"What's the matter?" shrieked the old woman

The young man of the ornate boots and gaudy hand-kerchief staggered in at the cabin door and slumped to the floor.

"Cleechie!" cried Mahala. "What's the matter with you?"

"I'm shotten right smart," said Cleech weakly.

"Git him over thar on the pallet, quick, Ad."

They put Cleech on the dirty pallet, and Mahala began looking for the trouble. It was not hard to find. Two bullets had struck him, but neither had entered the rib cavity. He need not have been in danger, if a skilled surgeon could have got to him at once. But while he was dragging himself three miles over the rough hog-back, every drop of blood had tried to run out of his body. His clothing was saturated with it.

"Good Lord, Ad!" moaned Mahala in despair. "I don't know what to do. I'll run—"

Cleech lay with his eyes closed, muttering: "Bound to

have been that heller, Benton Vane. Couldn't nobody else
sling lead—"

"His mind's wanderin', Ad," whispered Mahala. "You
stay here, and I'll run get Angy Tebo. She's the handiest
person on Rollin' Fork in a case like this."

Mahala was out the door and gone for the Tebo cabin,
half a mile away. Cleech opened his eyes and looked up at
Ad March. "I ain't wandering in my mind at all. Hand me
that bottle of whisky off'n the shelf."

March handed him the open bottle, and he took a heavy
jolt of whisky.

"Better now," he went on. "As I was saying when mammy
went out, that heller, Bent Vane, is over at the old Vane
House."

"No," said March, "that can't be. You said Bent Vane was
killed at Tascosa, and buried on Boot Hill."

"Aw, heck, Uncle Ad. Can't a feller lie, without having it
throwed up to him? I know what I told mammy. She has
made me tell that lie a thousand times. It was thisaway.
Mammy has been set on getting what she calls her rights,
all her life. She brang me up on the story of Randall Vane's
gold, and told me always that half of it was hers by rights.

"After pappy died, me and her picked cotton and saved
enough to buy me a full-rigged saddle, chaps, boots,
spurs, and everything. Full cowboy outfit. Then, when I
was sixteen, she sent me out to the plains country, to be a
cowboy, and hunt Bent Vane, and kill him. For eight year
I went into every hell-hole in the cow country, looking for
Bent Vane. Then one day I found him—but I didn't kill
him. Didn't even try. He wasn't in Tascosa, nohow, and—"

"Where was he?"

"Never mind where he was. I found out he had a big ranch, and about a million horses and cattle, and—I found out something else. Benton Vane ain't just what the ignorant hill-billies call a heller. He's a real heller. I seen him in action just one time, and that was enough for me. A gang of rustlers had been burning some Flying V cows. One day a dozen of them rustlers were in the old Tiger's Claw Saloon, at— No matter, I ain't telling where it was. Gimme that whisky again."

CLEECH TOOK ANOTHER man-size drink, and went on: "As I was saying, a dozen of 'em was in the saloon, and I was in there, too. Bent Vane, the handsomest man I ever seen in my life, walks in. His yaller hair is shining, and his blue eyes stabs like the devil's pitchfork. He's got two guns on him, and he stands right up in the open and whips them rustlers cold. When the smoke clears away, six of 'em are on the floor dead, and others are gone. Then he looks at me, scrooched down in a corner and scared to death.

" 'You belong to that outfit?' he asks me. I tell him no, I don't. 'Maybe you don't,' he says. 'Just look around you and see what happens to 'em when they burn the brand on a Flying V. Come on and take a drink.' I taken that drink with Benton Vane, and I don't want to take no more with him, nor do nothing else with him. I don't want to try to kill him, either."

"I see," said Ad March, trying to wet his dry lips with his tongue, "but he were killed, weren't he?"

"No. All the killing he ever got was what I done with my tongue. Mammy had deviled me to death to kill him, and I really meant to kill him, until I seen him, and then—I changed my mind. So, I fixed up that lie and told it to

Mammy. I told it the same way until she believed it, and I almost believed it myself. I never knowed why Mammy hated Benton Vane so. She hated all the Vanes worse than the devil, but she hated Benton more than all the rest put together, and couldn't rest until she thought he was dead."

"I reckon I know," said Ad March, "and I don't blame her none. She knowed Benton Vane when he was hellin' around Vaneburg, with gold money in every pocket. When he was goin' to dances on Rollin' Fork, and pretendin' that he didn't think he was any better than the Rollin' Fork folks. The women was all crazy about him, and he had his own way with them, damn his handsome soul! But, no matter now. That's all past. What makes you think Benton Vane is at the old Vane House?"

"Because they ain't nary 'nother man on earth that can sling that much lead that quick, and hit me twice at that distance. But, Uncle Ad, don't you ever tell Mammy that Benton Vane ain't dead. Women can't understand such things. It does her a lot of good to think Bent's dead. Let her go on thinking it. She hated Franklin Vane, too. She sung for an hour after I told her I had plugged him. Oh, well. I've worked pretty hard to get Mammy's rights. I reckon I got the last one of the Vanes to-night. When Mammy, gets old Randall Vane's gold, we'll go some place—some place—"

Cleech's voice trailed off, and he closed his eyes. March spoke to him, but he didn't answer. Then the postmaster put a finger on the boy's pulse. He felt it flutter, halt, flutter again, then stop. He laid the limp, clammy hand down, and growled:

"Huh! You have already went some place."

HALF AN HOUR later the two women came in. Mahala took one look at the cold, gray face on the pallet, then screamed. That wild scream was more than grief. It contained every weird note of grief, rage and hate. It was blood-curdling. She dropped to a seat on one of the boxes. Her mouth was a straight, hard line. There were no tears.

"Well, he's gone," she said, after a while, "but not before he kilt Franklin Vane, and I reckon he got the girl to-night. I told him to get her. That leaves only the old woman between me and my rights. She won't be in the way long. I'll tear her to pieces with my own hands, if there is no other way."

"Looks to me you're talkin' right smart, Mahala," said March.

"Angy knows my rights," answered Mahala. "She's a Chaffin, before she married a Tebo. She ain't goin' to talk outside."

"No, you bet I ain't, Mahala. I know yo' rights as well as what anybody knows 'em. You'd ort to be sittin' in the old Vane House in silks and satins, eatin' out'n silver and drinkin' out'n gold. You would be, too, if'n you had half yo' rights."

The night was growing chilly. Ad March made a little fire in the fireplace. The two women filled their clay pipes, and Ad took a liberal chew of home-grown twist. Thus they kept the vigil. From time to time a few low words were spoken, but for most part they were silent.

Mahala's face was as hard and expressionless as granite. No one would have guessed, by looking at her face, the terrible storm that was going on in her mind, and in what answered for her heart. The frightful vengeance that she was planning for her son, who was the only thing on earth that she had ever loved, and him only as an animal loves its offspring.

Long before daylight, Ad March rose and took a fresh chew. Then, without looking at Mahala, he said:

"Well, Mahaly, I got to get back over the ridge, in time to open the post office, and all."

Without looking up or turning her head, Mahala spat at him:

"Adam March, less'n they got post offices in hell, you're apt to be out'n a job pretty soon."

SO SAT THE two watch parties. One in a palace and the other in a hovel, the two connected by a tie of which Price Stanley and Myra Vane were all unaware, as they sat in the great parlor, speaking a few low words from time to time, and watching the light in the tall windows turn from pearl to pink in the dawn. The two old men dozed a little in the late hours of the night, and the early morning. They knew a great many things, but they were wise old men, and taciturn.

Old Peg Short had not told Price all he knew. Price's summing up of the situation, with Adam March as the principal villain, had awakened a whole school of memories in the mind of the old cobbler. He had thought of many things through that long, silent night.

The history of the House of Vane was an open book to Old Dr. Potts. He had been born in Vaneburg, as Old Peg Short had been. His professional errands had taken him to many strange places. He had heard odd bits of gossip, and had plenty of time to piece them together while he fished in the roistering Paramo, and shot squirrels from the tall trees of the bottoms. He and Peg Short had been much together, for there was no one else about Vaneburg who would be company to either of them.

Both these old men knew the hill people, and all their peculiarities. Both knew that a storm would break when Rolling Fork learned that a Perkins and another Tebo had been killed. Neither of them blamed Price, but the fact remained that he had slain a Perkins and a Tebo. Neither of the old men knew just where this murderous onslaught on the Vanes could be coming from. Both could guess shrewdly, and keep their guesses to themselves.

Candy Troboy had gone on to his father's home, and had told the news. He was a sad and wounded messenger of defeat, but he could still talk, and he took pains to hold Ad March up for what he was, in his recital of the events at Vaneburg that morning.

Long before Cleech Feeters stumbled into the cabin at the head of the draw, the story had spread up and down Rolling Fork like fire in dry stubble. A wagon, manned by Perkinses and Tebos, had driven from lower Rolling Fork around to Vaneburg. As they passed along the opposite side of the river, the men in the wagon could see the gray old mill and the grim Vane House, perched on its bluff. They shook their fists and cursed the place bitterly.

When Ad March reached his store at daylight, he peered into the little house at the back of the store. The coffins were gone, and Ad was glad of it. He had been a fool, he told himself, to let Mahala pull him into this mess. He would rather have a whole skin than all of Randall Vane's gold. He didn't blame Mahala for hating the Vanes, but she was a fool to think she could whip them. Champions of that strange family seemed to rise out of the very earth. What if Benton Vane was back there? All the men on Rolling Fork wouldn't be a breakfast spell for Bent, if he was as bad as Cleech said he was.

But Cleech could lie. Had lied. Had admitted on his deathbed that he had lied to his mother. Perhaps he had lied about seeing Benton Vane. Still, it would be well enough to stay on the safe side, and keep to his store and post office.

At thought of the post office, Mahala's last remark about post offices in hell slapped him in the face like a blow. What had she meant? Was she holding him responsible for Cleech's death? Would she throw him if the law took a hand in the matter? He knew she would, and he knew she had all the evidence needed to break his neck.

"Post offices in hell," he muttered, and slunk into his store. If anybody dragged him farther into that mess, they'd have to come into the post office to get him, and he'd set the government on them. Then he thought of Price Stanley kicking him into the street, and quivered with rage and fear, but fear was the dominant emotion.

BY MID FORENOON, three graves were being opened in the graveyard near the little Rolling Fork meeting house. One of them was for Silas Perkins, the Lord's anointed avenger; one for Asa Tebo; and the third for Cleechie Feeters, who had died like a Texan with his ornate boots on.

A considerable crowd of dour-faced men had gathered to dig the graves. Far out to one side two people sat on a fallen log. One of them was old Parson Chaffin, in his long-tailed coat. The other was Mahala Feeters. She wore no bonnet and her black hair glistened in the sun. She scorned headcovering as an Indian would. She had looked so long at the sun-baked ground of Texas that she could look the puny sun of Missouri in the eye and never flinch.

"Listen to me, Lige Chaffin," she was saying. "You're a Chaffin, and you used to be a man before you got smart enough to hide behind that long-tailed coat and a Bible. I ain't askin' you to fight. All I'm askin' is that you make Rollin' Fork take the Vane House apart, kill that cattle drover, or whoever it is that kilt Sile and Asa and my Cleechie. I'll go with 'em. I'll be the first one into the house. All I ask is that you rile 'em, and make 'em wild to go, an' revenge—"

"Vengeance is mine, saith the Lord," rumbled the old parson. "Don't you know the scriptur', sister?"

"Shet up! Don't you 'sister' me, you damned old hypocrite. I'm tellin' you what I want did, and you're goin' to do it. I've been in Texas a spell, but I've got a good memory. I know what went with that Yankee tin-peddler that was out of pocket year or two before I left here. I know all about Ailsy Whitfield that was, and plenty more. A real preacher is the greatest sort of man on earth. Nobody's above 'em, except God. Nobody's below a hypocrite like you except the Devil, and you run him clost for the bottom seat. You'll either do what I say, or you'll leave Rollin' Fork so quick you'll forget yo' Bible and run clean out'n that long-tailed coat of yo'n."

"Come, come, Mahala. Don't get so personal and explicit. Tell me what it is you want did, and I'll do it if I can."

"Oh, you can do it! The Devil put a tongue in yo' head that can make a fool of a man as well as it can of a woman. I want you to rile 'em, when you go to preach them funer-als. Pull that stately-steppin' and Lord's anointed stuff, like you did at Malvin's funeral. You riled 'em then. You got three funerals, and ort to rile 'em three times as much. It ort to be easy for you. You know that old Anson Vane skint yo' granddaddy out'n the mill site. You know the Vanes wouldn't spit on a Chaffin, or throw a dawg-bone to a Tebo, a Perkins, a Troboy, or a Feeters. You know—"

"I'll do my best, sister."

"You'd better, and remember this. If yo' best ain't good enough to make the Rollin' Fork men go with me and take that cattle drover, my best is goin' to be good enough to make 'em go with Pike Haney and make you set yo' ankles afire gettin' out'n this country."

MAHALA, A RAGING virago now, had fired her parting shot and had seen Parson Chaffin wince. She rose and walked away, with her head up like a grenadier. She knew her man. She knew the old rascal was not a minister of the gospel. She had once heard a real preacher ask him where he was ordained, and he replied:

"Why, I ain't been ordained, brother, by no certain sect. I just taken up preachin' and gives the word as I sees it."

As the virago walked away, the parson muttered to himself:

"Not much Chaffin in Mahala. Part old Anson Vane, but mostly the Devil. Well, she wants 'em riled; I guess I better rile 'em. No tellin' how it 'll end up, but anything is better than havin' trouble with Mahaly Feeters. I heard a feller say one time that two thoroughbreds produce a thorough-bred, two scrubs produce a scrub, and a thoroughbred and a scrub might produce anything, even the devil. Lem was a scrub, Ca'line was a thoroughbred, and Mahaly is mighty close to the Devil, when she's riled."

All Rolling Fork was at that funeral, and Parson Chaffin kept his word. He "riled 'em." The very earth shook with his denunciation of the slayers of the three men he was burying. He knew that every one of them was bent on murder when he was killed, but that made no difference to Parson Chaffin. He was inciting them to riot, murder, and arson; not that he cared anything about the matter involved, but to save himself from the wrath of Mahala Feeters.

After the funeral the men gathered in knots and groups. Mahala went from one to another of these groups, and spoke four words to each:

"My cabin at dark."

10

TO ESCAPE

AT DAYLIGHT THAT morning, Price Stanley left Myra in the big parlor long enough to hold a consultation with the two old men in the library.

"Gentlemen," he said, "it is clear enough to all of us that an attempt is being made to wipe out the Vane family, and it has almost succeeded. The bullet that killed Mrs. Vane was intended for Myra. It is useless to stay here and see her murdered, and we seem to be powerless to stop them. Can't I get another horse somewhere, and take Myra out of it all?"

"You wouldn't get five miles until you'd both be dead," said Peg Short.

"But they only operate at night," objected Price.

"They started a right nice operation on you yesterday mornin'," said Peg. "It wasn't a success, but they started it. The next time they'll operate with squirrel rifles and Navy six-shooters, and it'll be a complete success."

"H'm, h'm! Yes. They operated on Cap'n Vane in the daytime, too. H'm! The operation was a beautiful success, but the patient died. Yes. Something you haven't thought of. Myra could get away better by herself than she could with you."

"What do you mean by that?" asked Price, his eyes kindling with resentment.

"H'm, h'm! Just what I say. Somebody is tryin' to clean up the Vane family. There are only two or three of them, likely. By this time, every man on Rollin' Fork and in the hills around here is out to clean you up."

"I hadn't thought of that," said Price.

"Better think of it," Peg Short said, "There would be a mighty slim, doubtful chance for Myra to ride away from here, but not in the daytime. There is no chance at all for you to get away, either night or day."

"You paint it pretty dark," said Price.

"It is dark," replied Peg. "Doc and I knew it was dark, when we brought our guns here. We're willin' to stick the thing out with you and Myra, and maybe when night comes, you can get away, but not now."

"All right, you two know these people better than I do. I have just one thing to say. I know that Myra is in danger of death every moment, and I won't leave her, no matter what happens."

"H'm, h'm! Spoken like a gentleman. Don't blame you a darn' bit."

"We've got to get Mrs. Vane buried some way," said Peg Short. "I don't know whether it'll be safe to go to Vaneburg for a coffin or not. If it is, I don't know whether anybody'll dig a grave or not."

"H'm. Dog won't bite a doctor. I'll go over and see about it. Got to have some breakfast first. You and Myra see if you can find something to eat. Come on, Peg. Let's look around a bit."

Price and Myra went down to the kitchen. The doctor

and old Peg Short went to the mill yard. Price had told them about seeing the man fall and roll down the hill. They went to the head of the steps and stopped. There was no man in sight, either dead or alive, but there was something on the big flat rock besides the two fish poles and a bait can. One thing was a new .38 rifle. The other was blood. In fact, there was blood all down the steps and clear across the rock.

"H'm, h'm, h'm. If we had a good dog, I believe we could ketch that feller, Peg." The doctor looked up at the distance from where they stood to the back yard gate. "There's been some fancy shootin' here."

NOT WISHING TO follow the trail of blood farther just then, they picked up the rifle and turned back toward the house. Suddenly, the doctor stopped and looked at Peg Short.

"Peg, that ain't a Missouri gun. They don't use 'em here. That come from Texas, or out West."

"Reckon so," said Peg. "I never saw one like it before."

"H'm! Peg— Did you know that Mahala Chaffin was back on Rollin' Fork?"

"No!"

"Yes, she is. I heard that fool Dacy Blodgett and his wife talkin' in the kitchen while I was eatin' breakfast yesterday mornin'. They said Mahala was at the funeral, bold as life, and puttin' on airs like she was a full-blooded Vane, instead of only a half-breed. They said Mahala's boy, Cleech, was with her struttin' around in high-heel boots like—"

"Hold the deal, doc. Don't gimme no more cards until I play what I got. High-heel boots—Texas rifle. I told

you about them tracks. Do you reckon that Cleech boy
would—"

"H'm! I don't know. If I had thought he'd ever do a thing
like that, I'd 'a' let him die with membranous croup when
he was a kid. I would, damn him!"

"You—you know what they said about Benton Vane and
Mahala Chaffin, when—"

"Yes!" snapped the doctor, forgetting to hum. "I know
more about it then anybody that lives, and I know most
of it was lies. I know Bent was a heller. Franklin Vane left
him here with two old niggers, clean through the war. He
was about grown, had money in every pocket, and of course
he went to the devil. He romped all up and down Rollin'
Fork, but—"

"Well, there was talk of him and Mahala marryin', even
if he was about a second cousin."

"Yes, and most of the talkin' was done by the Chaffins
and the Tebos. They wanted to marry back into the Vane
money. Mahala was willin' enough. She never had as much
blood in her as a sucker fish. She inherited the cold-blood-
edness of old Anson Vane and the sorry damn' meanness of
the Chaffins. Then when Benton Vane went away, Mahala
and her tribe set up a yell that Bent had promised to marry
her and then ditched her. It was every word lies. I know
just what made Bent leave here."

"What was it, doc?"

"H'm, h'm! This is between you and me, Peg, of course.
When Captain Franklin Vane came back here after the
war and found out what a heller Bent was, he went wild
and tried to stop the boy all at once. About the first thing
Franklin Vane heard was that Bent was fixin' to marry

Mahala Chaffin. The Cap'n went crazy. He called Bent on
the carpet, and Bent told me just what happened. I loaned
the boy a thousand dollars to go to Texas on. I thought it
was mighty little, but I learned afterward that he could
have bought the whole damned State at that time for half
of it."

"What did Bent say happened?"

"Why, Bent laughed about it. He said the old man called
him into the library, serious as a drunk owl, and shut the
door. He thought the Cap'n was goin' to ride him about
not gettin' along with Matilda. But the old man pushes
a spring in a table and two loaded derringers jumps out
in front of him. He picks 'em up and says, 'Benton, if you
marry Mahala Chaffin, I'm going to kill you with one of
these, and myself with the other.'

"It made Bent mad, of course, and he snaps back, 'I'm not
going to marry Mahala, because I don't want to be killed
with one of 'em, but I don't care a damn how soon you kill
yourself with the other one.'"

"Huh! That's what all the fuss was made over?"

"Yes, that was it. Bent pulled out to Texas, and I reckon
forgot it, because he sent Myra to the old man when his
wife died. I reckon Cap'n Vane forgave Bent, because he
raised the girl and done all he could for her."

"Reckon the Cap'n never heard from Bent?"

"Nobody on earth ever knew anything about Captain
Vane's affairs, since he came back from the war. He didn't
talk. I heard from Benton Vane, two years after he left here.
He sent me twelve hundred dollars. The thousand I loaned
him, and ten per cent interest for two years. Benton Vane
was wild and spoilt, when he was a boy, but he was as square

as a die and as smart as Randall Vane ever was. Bent would fight hell with a gill of water if he thought he was right, and he'd stand up for himself anywhere."

"HUH! THAT'S THE way it was, eh? Well, that don't help us none in straightenin' out this mess. Doc, if Mahala is back here, everybody on Rollin' Fork is kin to her on the Chaffin side. Sile Perkins and Asa Tebo were both kin to her. If she puts old Anson Vane's brains to work—look out!"

"That's just what I was thinkin' about when I told young Price he couldn't get away from here. Rollin' Fork is goin' to get him."

"Looks like it, doc. Pity, too. He's a fine young feller, and the best fighter I ever seen. It throws you and me in a pretty bad mess, but I'm goin' to stay with him."

"H'm! I'll stay with him as long as I got a bullet, a cap, and a spoonful of powder. Partly on his account. Partly because Bent Vane's girl thinks a lot of him. If we can manage to get 'em out of these hills and onto his own prairie, he'll take care of Myra for good and all."

"I believe he would, doc. Seems to me he likes her right well."

"Likes her, you blamed old fool! He's crazy about her, and I don't blame him. She's the prettiest thing I ever saw in my life. I don't blame her, either; he's a mighty good figure of a man."

"Yes, we got to get 'em out of here some way, doc. It don't make much difference about you and me. We're dead old. But it would be a shame for a fine boy and girl like that to be butchered before they even had a good look at life."

"H'm! Yes, it would, Peg. We got to get 'em out, for it's goin' to happen to-night. Lark Feeters was so 'fraid of a

Vane that he slept in a tree, with a ring of fire around it, but Lark's dead, and Mahala ain't afraid of the Devil himself. If it's her that's ram-roddin' this thing, and it looks like that, she can make Rollin' Fork do anything. First thing, we got to bury that woman. Then we've got to figure out some way to get Price and Myra away from here as soon as it gets dark, or we'll all be killed in a pile. Let's go eat."

AFTER BREAKFAST DR. POTTS slipped his "irons" into the waistband of his pantaloons, got in his old buggy, and rattled off to town. In an hour he was back. Said he had fed Price's horse and had put his own saddle horse in the rock stable and fed it.

"We'll find a way to get 'em out when night comes, Peg. Then Price and Myra will just have to ride and take a chance. It's a mighty slim chance, but it's the only one they'll have."

"Yes, but, doc, you forgot what you went to town for."

"No, I didn't. Live people are always more important to me than dead ones, so I mentioned Price and the girl first. I got a coffin, and I got four fellows to dig the grave. They didn't want to do it, but I told 'em I'd poison every damn' one of 'em the first time they got sick if they didn't. H'm! I told you a dog wouldn't bite a doctor. There they come now."

A wagon drove up; the coffin was carried in.

"Dig that grave right by the side of the captain's grave," ordered Dr. Potts, "so he'll have a wife on each side of him. Looks like a dirty trick to play on a dead man, to me, but then I'm a bachelor. It may be all right."

Mrs. Vane was put in her coffin, just as she was. Then the coffin was placed on two chairs in the little boudoir.

Few people ever lie in state in richer or more beautiful surroundings.

After that, Myra and the three men returned to the parlor and went into committee of the whole house.

"Price," said Peg Short, "doc and I have decided that you and Myra have got to ride from here as soon as it gets dark. We had just as well face what we're up against. I'm not sayin' you did wrong when you shot Sile and Asa apart. It was the only thing you could do and get out of it alive yourself. But the fact remains that you killed 'em. Three of us can't hold this house against an army, and that's what it'll be. A howlin' mob. I've seen Rollin' Fork riled before. They probably won't do much to-day, they'll be busy with the buryin', but when night comes—"

"I think you're right," said Price. "Can you ride a horse, Myra?"

"I don't know," Myra hesitated. "I rode some at school, but— If the horse was gentle, I wouldn't fall off."

"Of course you wouldn't," hummed Dr. Potts. "I've got a horse for you that's as gentle as a kitten and as fast as a blue streak. All you'll have to do will be to hang on and follow Price. It's not a question of whether you want to go or not. You've got to take that chance, or—none."

"Oh, I'll go," said Myra. "Anything to get away from this terrible place."

"All right," Peg grunted, "that's settled, and you'll have all day to get ready. Price, you said you wouldn't leave Myra for anything. Stay right with her. Doc and I will look after the grave diggin' and get everything ready."

THE CONFERENCE BROKE up. Price and Myra went back to the parlor. He had reloaded the two revolvers and had them on his person. It irked him to be hiding there in the house while the doctor and Peg Short were exposing themselves to whatever danger there might be in the daytime. But he knew some one was trying to kill Myra, and she meant more to him now than everything else on earth. Nothing could make him get very far from her.

"Price," said Myra in a low tone, "grandmother had a small bag packed and was getting ready to go somewhere. Do you think she was in collusion with—those who killed grandfather, and that they killed her by mistake?"

"I don't know what to think, Myra. I am sure that the one who killed her thought he was shooting at you. I would rather not think she was a party to a murder plot. Let's try to believe that she was slightly unbalanced, terribly frightened, and was trying to make her escape in some way."

"You are right, Price. I'm glad we're going away. I feel that when I get out on those wild prairies I'll be free. I don't know where I'll go, but I'll be away from this terrible house."

Price looked at her. This was no time or place to tell her what was in his mind. Anyway, they might never win out of those hills. She would be with him. He would tell her before the last, if they fell into the hands of the Rolling Fork men, because he wanted her to know that he loved her.

Neither Price nor the girl knew the pitch to which the rage of those hill people could be aroused. Neither of them knew anything about Mahala Feeters and her son from Texas. Price knew nothing of the history of the Vanes except the little that Peg had told him. Myra knew little more.

The two old men knew many things, and their faces were grave as they moved restlessly about the place, ever watchful. It was mid-afternoon when the grave was finished. Two of the four men who had helped dig it took the wagon and went back to town. The other two came to the house and stood hat in hand on the portico, with the red clay on their cowhide boots.

"H'm, h'm! Two of the diggers slipped away. Guess I'll have to poison 'em next time they're sick, like I told 'em. Didn't mean for you to leave the house, Price. Looks like you'll have to—"

"I won't leave Myra in the house alone," said Price flatly.

"She'll have to go, anyway," said Peg. Custom was riding Peg Short's mind at that moment. Six pallbearers were the custom. He and the doctor and the two hillmen could have carried the casket easily, but in his mind there must be six.

SO THE PROCESSION moved off toward the grave. The two hillmen, with their clayey boots, leading; Peg Short on one side and Dr. Potts on the other, at the middle handles; while Price and Myra carried the remaining two.

At the south side of the yard was a gate through which all the Vanes since old Anson had passed at the start of the last journey. They passed through it and on to the open grave.

In addition to the feeling of depression in the presence of death, four of those pall-bearers had other things on their minds. There before them were the pick, the spade, and the open grave, long recognized as the emblems of death, and they bore food for that open mouth of earth, but they were not thinking of these things. Their nerves were tensed and their ears strained for the crack of a rifle from some copse of the woods.

None came. A Sabbath silence was over the place. They placed the coffin in the grave and the two men set to filling it. Myra leaned against a flat tombstone at the grave on the opposite side of Captain Vane's cloddy coverlet of clay, while Price stood beside her. The inscription on that slab of marble read: "Sacred to the memory of Myra Calfus Vane, wife of Benjamin Franklin Vane. Born June 10, 1823. Died October 12, 1859."

"My own grandmother," whispered Myra, pointing to the inscription. "I was named after her."

Price took the shovel to relieve one of the men. Myra watched the play of his powerful shoulders as he wielded the shovel.

As soon as the grave was filled, the two men caught up their tools and walked away in unseemly haste. They climbed the fence and took the old Red Road toward Vaneburg.

"Afraid of a Vane, even when he's dead," said Peg Short.

"There's no other kind to be afraid of now," replied Dr. Potts. "We'd better get back to the house."

THEY TURNED AWAY from the graves, then stopped. Three men had stopped a hundred feet away at the old worm fence, and were looking at them. The sun glinted on pistols at their belts.

"Here's where it happens," growled Peg Short, and went for his gun.

"No, wait!" snapped Dr. Potts, his "h'm" not working. "They're not hill people. What the devil are they, anyway? I never saw—"

The men were mounted. They wore broad hats, and their faces were tanned. One of them dismounted and climbed the vine-grown fence. He was a tall, slender man, who walked with a springy step that made his spurs clink as he approached the party at the grave.

Myra still leaned against her grandmother's stained tombstone, as if to find solace there, and Price stood beside her. They were several paces from Peg and the doctor, who were between them and the approaching stranger.

He came on without looking up until he was within twenty feet of the two old men, then he stopped, removed his hat in the presence of a woman and out of deference to the new grave. The sun flashed on his golden hair and glinted in his sea-blue eyes.

"Benton Vane!" gasped Peg Short in amazement.

"Yes, I'm Benton Vane, and— Why, hello, Peg!" He caught the old man's hand. "And this is Dr. Potts. You two have lasted well. What—what is the occasion here?" He pointed to the two new graves.

"One of them is your father," replied the doctor. "The other one is your—his wife."

"So lately," said Benton Vane in a subdued tone. "Father wrote some time ago that he was getting feeble, but he made no mention that the madame was— I had hoped to get here before father— But death doesn't wait."

"No," said Dr. Potts, gravely. "We buried your father the day before yesterday. We have just finished filling Mrs. Vane's grave."

Myra's face was veiled, but she was looking at this stranger through her veil, and Price was staring openly. With his golden hair slightly curled at the ends, and the light in his blue eyes, Benton Vane was still the perfect counterpart of that picture in the library, that now had a bullet in the forehead. Vane was then forty-eight years old, but looked not more than thirty-five.

"And who are these young people?" he asked, waving his broad hat toward Price and Myra.

"This is Mr. Price Stanley." He shook hands with Price. "The young lady is—your daughter, Myra Vane."

"Myra!" cried Benton Vane. "Take off the veil and let me see what you look like."

Never were two faces more alike. Myra didn't go to her father's arms, though she wanted to. He made no move to embrace her, though his heart was hungering. He stood and looked at her, with wonder in his eyes.

"Tell me, tell me, tell me," he said.

"There's too much to tell you here," said Peg Short, who had recovered from his surprise long enough to think of the possibility of a rifle shot from out there in the woods. "Let's go to the house."

11

TEXAS GUNS

BENTON VANE WAVED an arm at the two men he had left in the road, and they moved on down to the yard gate with Vane's horse. As they turned toward the gate that led into the yard, Benton Vane fell in by the side of Myra.

"So this is the little baby girl that I sent home! It doesn't seem so long ago, but now you're a grown woman." They entered the yard, and Vane went on. "I can't go in just yet. Wait here for me."

Benton Vane strode to the front gate. He jerked it open, caught the bridle of his horse. Then Benton Vane committed a desecration. The horse, a beautiful bay, with high head and flashing eyes, was led through that gate and onto the blue-grass turf, which no iron-shod beast had ever trod before.

The man seemed to have forgotten everything else on earth but what he was doing. He dropped the bridle rein on the ground, and the horse sidled away from him and stopped.

A wagon rattled by. It had the sheet down from the front bows, and a brown man sat on the seat driving the four mules. He was calling in a strange language to the four who stood under the walnut tree, watching the queer events that were taking place. Following the wagon came a long string of horses, trotting along. Each of them had what looked like a piece of frazzled rope about its neck. They were hobbles, which the four watchers had never seen before, and the use of which they knew nothing about.

"Peg," called Benton Vane, in a sharp tone that rang with command, "where is the nearest ford on the Paramo?"

"One five mile down the river, and another three mile above here," replied Peg.

"Has that old bridge got a floor in it?"

"Yes, I reckon so," replied Peg. "It had one when I crossed it this mornin'."

"All right, boys!" snapped Vane. "We'll have to cross 'em on the bridge. Here, one of you take this horse and buggy through that gate, into the clover patch. Then you two get on to the bridge and get ready to point 'em. We'll have to water on the other side; bank on this side is fifty feet high. Don't let 'em run. Why the hell don't some more pointers come on here? Don't you let 'em crowd, or they'll bust that old bridge wide open."

Price, Myra, Peg and the doctor stood under that old tree, watching in amazement. A Vane using such language in the presence of a woman was unthinkable. The fact was, Benton Vane would not have used such language in the presence of any woman, but at that moment he didn't realize that there was a woman within miles of him. He was out on the wide plains working cattle, with no woman near. All of his mind, except that pertaining to cattle, was blank for the moment.

The puzzled watchers of this strange performance had forgotten all about the danger of rifle shots. Benton Vane's orders were cracking like rifle shots themselves, and were being obeyed with alacrity, but what on earth was the man talking about?

A dozen more of those strange riders in their wide hats, with tanned faces, their leather breeches flapping, guns at their belts and ropes coiled at their saddle-horns, came dashing along the road. They looked all bundled up to Price and Myra, but they seemed to feel quite free. They checked as they came opposite Vane, and he called out to them:

"Get on to the bridge, and point 'em. Begin to string 'em at the mouth of the lane."

IT WAS QUITE clear, now, to the group under the tree that Benton Vane was crazy. They couldn't see anything to point. No one had been fishing, and there was nothing to string.

Vane was paying no more attention to them than if they had not been on earth. He poured some tobacco into a piece of paper, rolled it, and put it into his mouth. Then he applied a match, took a few quick puffs, and the thing seemed to have gone out. A moment later, he took the thing from his mouth and threw it on the ground. Then smoke began to pour from Vane's mouth, nose and apparently his eyes. Certainly the man was on fire. It was the first time that little group of people had ever seen a man roll a cigarette and inhale the smoke.

"H'm! Fire in the magazine. Blow up directly. Better stand back." The doctor had finally understood the amazing spectacle, and made his usual joke of it.

No one was listening to him. A strange sound was coming up the Red Road from the south. It was a low rumble, shot with a clattering, knocking sound. High above the general noise there stood out a strange note:

"Hoo-o-o-o! Hoo-o-o-o-o!"

Presently the strangest procession of the many strange ones that had passed the old Red Road came into view. Two more of those odd riders, on wiry little horses, were dancing down the road like twin drum-majors gone mad. While the horses whirled and danced, caracoled and curvetted, the men waved one hand and called:

"Hoo-o-o-o-o! Hoo-o-o-o-o-o! Hoo-o-o-o-o!"

"What now?" It was Peg Short who spoke.

"H'm! Don't ask me. Been wondering that myself. There's a chance for a new hunting horn, Peg. Look at 'em!"

Behind those dancing men came a solid wall of great, twisting horns, that reached from one side of the lane to the other. The twin drum-majors seemed to be putting on a special performance to show their skill, as they came opposite Benton Vane.

"Hold 'em!" he yelled. "Damn you, don't you let 'em run! They'll tear that old bridge to splinters, and kill the whole damned herd."

The drum-majors danced by, and the stream of cattle swept on after them. A few minutes later a new sound arose. It was the steady roar of thousands of hoofs on the old covered bridge. Once a beast was on that bridge, there was no danger to it. The bridge was housed in, with small windows high from the floor. The animal could do nothing but trot on through the long, dark tunnel.

Those skillful trail drivers, on their dancing horses, pinched the head of the big herd and let them trickle onto the bridge in a thin stream. The wide lane in front of the house choked up with a sea of horns. It was evident that the two drum-majors were "holding 'em."

Not once did Benton Vane take his eye off that herd until the last pair of long horns had gone on toward the bridge. Then he called to one of the men that were behind the herd:

"All right, Steve. They'll water on the other side. Take charge of the outfit. You'll find an open place about the size of a blanket two miles farther on. You'll have to bed 'em there to-night. If you want me, you'll find me here."

Steve Bradley, the trail boss, rode on after the cattle, while Benton Vane walked over to the group under the big tree.

"DON'T THINK I wasn't glad to see you, Myra," he said, "because I haven't paid more attention to you. When the time comes to work cattle, they have to be worked. There's seventy-five thousand dollars in that string of hoofs and horns, if I can get them to the Missouri River cornfields."

"I can understand that," said Price. "I brought a herd up the Red Road a day or two ago."

"Oh, you did?" said Vane. "How many?"

"A thousand," replied Price, proudly, for that was the biggest herd that had ever been up that trail, until the Texans came.

"A thousand!" There was a note of contempt in Vane's voice. "Why, that ain't a herd, that's a milk-bunch! There's five thousand in that little herd we brought up."

"Where on earth did you find that many cattle, Mr. Vane?" Price asked the Texan.

"Find 'em? Why, I rounded 'em off my range. There's only five thousand there. I was afraid to bring a big herd this way, and I'm glad I didn't. I intended to take ten thousand up the Chisum Trail, but the Cheyennes and Arapahoes are on the war path this spring. I had these five thousand contracted, so I brought them up this way, but I'll never try it again. The only thing we have had was plenty of water. I haven't seen any grass for four hundred miles. Those steers have lived on water, with a little sour dock, buck bushes and jack hickory leaves. I'd rather fight all the Indians in the country than drive this trail again."

"Well, we—we better get into the house," said Peg Short, thinking about rifle shots again.

"Yes. I want to see if the old place looks natural. Funny how these valleys have shrunk, and the hills settled since I have been away! Used to be big valleys in here, and now there is not room to turn around." Benton Vane led the way into the house with his daughter, and the others followed.

"H'm, h'm! Benton," said Dr. Potts, when they were all seated in the library, "I may as well tell you that your father was murdered."

"What! Murdered?" Benton Vane's blue eyes went dark.

"Yes, murdered, cold." The doctor went on to give Vane an account of the events of the last four days in detail. He told him that Price Stanley was a drover from the Blue Stem Country to the north, who was there by chance when the trouble started, and had stayed to help him and Peg protect the two women. He left out nothing, and he didn't let Price suffer in the report.

"Why, doctor, that's terrible!" said Vane, when the story was told. "If a thing like that happened in Texas or Kansas, nothing would be thought of it, but here in these old hills—"

"Bent, when the railroad ran through the country to the north of here, and another ran through the mountains to

the south, this part of the world was just forgotten. The
stage quit running on the old Red Road. Mail comes once
a week, on a mule. The country has gone back to the time
when old Anson Vane settled here. If there were a few
Indians, it would be just like Dan'l Boone found it, when
he used to come across from Kentuck' to hunt."

"Do you know who these killers are?" asked Vane.

"No, we don't. We have an idea who they might be, but—
Let Peg and me see you outside, Bent."

Benton Vane and the two old men left the library and
walked outside.

"Isn't he wonderful?" asked Myra.

"The handsomest man that I have ever seen in my life,"
replied Price. "No wonder you are beautiful. You are the
image of him."

Myra had not been fishing for that. She blushed and
looked out the window, while Price stood looking at her
with the light of love in his brown eyes.

"BENT," SAID THE old doctor, when they were outside,
"Mahala Feeters and her boy, Cleech, are back here from
Texas. Cleech wears high-heeled boots, and— You know
Mahala didn't like the Vanes much. Peg and I have been
tryin' to put things together, and it looks to us like—
Mahala is a cousin of yours, but—"

"I understand what you mean," said Benton Vane,
thoughtfully. "I saw Cleech Feeters out in Texas, and he
was in pretty bad company. I could have killed him easy
enough, and I guess I ought to have done it. He didn't
know that I knew who he was. I had Mahala and her boy
looked up down there. Meant to try to do something for
them, but I found out that they were a hard, hard lot, and

just let 'em alone. And now— A man can't help the kind of people that are kin to him. The Chaffins were bad blood. Lige was—"

"Steady, Bent. Lige is a preacher now."

"What! He was the rottenest heller on Rolling Fork when I was a boy, and a hog thief when I left here. I'll bet a hundred dollars he's a hypocrite."

"No doubt about that," drawled the doctor. "Just thought I'd tell you about him."

"As I was saying, all Chaffin blood is bad blood. That's why old Anson Vane raised such a smoke when Caroline married Lem Chaffin. He knew 'em. It did look pretty hard for Randall Vane to have so much, and Caroline have nothing. I always felt sorry for Mahala. That's why I noticed her, and that was why I had 'em looked up in Texas."

"Yes," said Old Peg, "and it looks to me like they are lookin' the Vanes up, now."

"Yes, it does look like that," said Benton Vane, musingly. "Mahala inherited some of Anson's brains, all of his bad traits, and none of his good ones. There was nothing but bad to inherit from the Chaffins."

"That's all true," said Dr. Potts, "but it can't be helped now. What I brought you out here for was to tell you this. Price Stanley killed Asa Tebo and Sile Perkins, and I've got an idea that he damn' nigh ruined Cleech Feeters last night. They're buryin' the dead ones over at Rollin' Fork, to-day. You know those people. They're goin' to get Price Stanley and they're goin' to get Myra if they stay here. Price has got a good horse over in Peg's stable, and I put my saddle horse in the stable with it. To-night, Peg and me aimed to get the boy and the girl on those horses, and let them make a run for it, before that Rollin' Fork gang comes to take this place apart and get everybody here."

"No!" snapped Benton Vane. "If that young chap wants to run, let him run, but that damned Rolling Fork rabble will never run my daughter away from her home! Since father is dead, this place belongs to me, and after me, it is Myra's. You can tell this young Stanley that—"

"Just a minute, Bent," said Dr. Potts. "I don't want you to get Price Stanley wrong. He could have gone on with his cattle, and let this mess go to the devil. Most men would have done it. If he hadn't stayed, we would have all been dead by this time. He'll stick as long as any man on earth, but—"

"All right, let him stick, then. Right here we'll stay, until we get a cold show-down. You two will stay with us, won't you?"

"Certainly," said the two old men, together.

"Good. What guns have you got?"

"Navy revolvers."

"What! Navies? Old cap-and-ball guns? Why—hasn't this country civilized any?"

"Not a damn' bit, Bent," drawled the doctor. "I'm still givin' the children santonin and lobelia, and the grown folks blue mass and powdered cinchona bark. They won't take nothin' else. The women still go to the creek to wash clothes, and the men still put the corn in one end of a sack, and a rock in the other, when they go to mill. What of it? It's just as good as any, if you don't know any better, and they don't."

"Maybe so," snapped Benton Vane, "but I know better. I'm going to my wagon and get some real guns. Then if the

Rolling Fork outfit comes here to-night, they'll get what's coming to them. If they don't come, I'll take two or three of my boys to-morrow and clean out the whole lot of them."

12

A HOUSE OF DREAD

BENTON VANE STRODE to his horse, led it outside, mounted, and galloped away down the road toward the bridge through which his cattle had been driven. They heard him clatter through it, and Dr. Potts said:

"H'm, h'm! Same old Bent. Still willin' to fight hell with a gill of water. Guess all we can do is sit tight and watch the fireworks."

A few minutes later Benton Vane was back. He had another pistol at his belt, and three, with their belts and holsters, hanging on the horn of his saddle. He passed them to Peg, and the weight of the heavy forty-fives almost pulled the old sheriff down.

"Here's cartridges," said Vane, as he tossed a bag of them on the ground inside the yard. "Now let 'em come, damn 'em! I would have brought some of my boys, but we won't need 'em. Anyway, there is a cloud coming up. If it rains, the cattle may run, and it will take all hands to handle them. Wait here until I put my horse in that clover patch."

He threw his saddle over the fence into the yard, and led his horse across the lane and through the gate. Then Peg and the doctor saw what that frazzled rope was for, as Vane hobbled the animal, so he could catch it when he wanted it.

"H'm, h'm! I was right glad to see Bent lookin' so well, and seemin' prosperous and all, but I think we would have been better off if he hadn't come until to-morrow. We might have got Price and the girl away to-night. As it is—h'm!"

"I wish he had brought a few of his boys," said Peg. "It's goin' to be right lonesome here for four men and one woman, if all Rollin' Fork comes to the party."

"H'm, yes, and they'll come, but you can't talk to Bent Vane. Never could talk to any Vane. All hot-headed fools. Well, it's his house, since the old cap'n is gone, and it's his girl. We delivered the house and the girl to him in good order, except that two windows are broke, and the girl's heart is gone. We are just as well off here as we would be in Vaneburg. Those devils will be after us."

TO DR. POTTS Benton Vane offered one of the heavy forty-fives.

"No, thank you, Bent," said the doctor. "I'll lay this handy, where I can get it as I pass, if I have to run, but I'd rather have my old irons while the loads last."

"Thank you, Bent," said Peg Short, returning the one he had accepted, "but them guns is too heavy for me. They'd bog my wooden leg before I could run fifty feet, and I'm right easy to skeer. I'll just use my old Navies while the loads last, then depend on my good leg and the pick-handle."

"All right. I'll give these other two to young Stanley. He's got ham enough to pack a pair of real guns."

They passed on into the house, and Benton Vane saw the two long forty-fives belted onto Price Stanley before he stopped. Then they all sat down in the library. Price felt

*Stanley emptied his
guns at the mob*

like a walking arsenal. He knew he would drown if he fell
into a foot of water. The Golden Derringers were in his
pockets. The two slender revolvers were in the waistband
of his trousers, hidden by his vest. Too much armament. He
was going to get rid of those revolvers at the first chance.

He was thinking of that when Benton Vane put his hand
under the table, pressed a spring, and the narrow drawer
shot out. It was empty. Price caught Myra's eye, and shook
his head.

"If you'll go down there and dredge the little pool where
you found father's body," said Benton Vane, "you will find

a pair of gold-mounted derringers. He shot himself and then fell into the pool."

"Here's the bullet that killed him," said Peg Short, producing the bullet. "Doc cut this out of the cap'n's back. Anyway, a derringer would have tore him in two. That bullet hole was too small to bleed. If the cap'n had killed himself, Malvin Tebo didn't kill himself, and Mrs. Vane didn't kill herself."

"I guess you are right," said Benton Vane. "Well, if they come back they will find one or two of the Vanes at home. Funny about that pair of derringers. Father always kept them in this drawer."

Again Myra looked at Price, and again he shook his head. She was taking orders only from him. He meant more to her than this strange father, whom she had never seen before that day. So she kept the derringers, and said nothing, as Bent went on:

"Well, we'd better eat something before night. Myra, can you rustle us a little grub?"

"Yes, I'll fix some supper," she said.

She and Price went out together.

"Is that young fellow a cook, too?" asked Benton Vane, with an odd, expression in his eyes.

"H'm, no," replied Dr. Potts. "He knows somebody is tryin' to kill Myra, and he won't let her get out of his sight, and—I don't think she wants to get out of his sight."

"Oh, it's like that," said Bent. "All in four days. Well, it was the same way with me and my wife, only it was just one day."

"These last four days have been right long ones," said Dr. Potts. "Long enough for Price to save Myra's life two-three times, and I think he aims to keep it saved. He's as clean a youngster as I ever saw."

"Oh, it's all right with me," said Benton Vane, nonchalantly. "Myra don't owe me anything that she knows of. Nothing but a few thousand dollars that I sent father from time to time to take care of her, and send her to school. I don't suppose he ever told her about that."

After supper, Bent insisted on a light in the library. Didn't propose to sit in a dark room, like a prairie dog in a hole, on account of a few hill-billies. They compromised on a lamp that was turned low and shaded. Price and Myra would have much preferred sitting on that couch in the parlor, but courtesy demanded that they sit in the room with the girl's father. The cloud was coming up, as Vane had predicted. Bent Vane got up and walked to the window, to look out at the threatening weather.

"Bent, you are courtin' death when you do that," said Doc Potts.

"I've courted it before," replied Bent, coolly, as he returned to his seat.

The rain began to fall, steadily, and without wind or lightning. The five of them sat in tense silence, listening. Myra wished she was near her big cattle drover, and could hold his hand. She would feel safer. She didn't think of her father as her protector.

NIGHTFALL HAD FOUND the Rolling Fork clans at Mahala's cabin, in answer to her call. She spoke to them briefly and grimly:

"To-night we're goin' to pay a debt to the Vanes that's been due for a long time. The Vane House is shelterin' the man that kilt Sile and Asa. My boy, Cleechie, tried to get that drover last night, and he shotten Cleechie until he bleeds to death."

Certainly Mahala knew she was lying. She had told Cleech to get Myra Vane, and she hoped he had done it.

She went on: "We'll take that drover to-night, and when we've got him we'll fix the Vane House and the old Vane Mill so's they'll never harbor another killer. We'll fix Peg Short so's he'll never sole another shoe, and Doc Potts so's he'll never roll another pill. I don't know the best way to go about it. If any of you got anything to say, say it. We ort to be goin'."

Old Hezzy Tebo got up. He was a little hump-shoul-dered runt, with a wisp of chin whiskers, but he had a big voice and four remaining sons, each of them over six feet.

"Mahaly, I recollect hearin' my grandpappy tell about the Osages jumpin' old Anson Vane one time. They went up the Paramo in canoes, and didn't make no noise. Anson whupped hell out'n 'em, because he had a passel of men and guns, and was lookin' for 'em. We know they's only three men at the Vane House. We kin raise a dozen boats. Some kin take 'em around the p'int, and the rest can cross the hog-back. Then when all's ferried across and landed below the mill's-tail, we can go in and help ourselves."

"Uncle Hezzy's got the right idea," said a dozen at once.

"Yes!" snapped Mahala, under her breath. "I gave it to him! Come on, then. Let's go and have it over with."

Mahala wore Cleech's boots, a pair of overalls and a shirt. She wore no hat, but a bandanna worn turban fashion held her black hair in place, and she looked like a pirate chief as she marshaled the Rolling Fork men over the hog-back to await the arrival of the boats.

Stalking along by her side was a man who would much rather have been somewhere else. Parson Chaffin had not known when he had "riled 'em" that day that he was going to march with this army. Mahala had not told him that till after the riling was done. Now, as they stumbled along in the dark, she hissed something in his ear.

"Remember the tin-peddler and Ailsy Whitfield. If you try to run, I'll shoot you if I swing for it. You're going to be into this as deep as I am, so you can't squeal on me, you dirty, double-crossin', split-tongued liar. You talked about a shield and buckler, while you was rilin' 'em to-day. I'm goin' to use you for one, and if you so much as reach out a hand to take anything you take a fancy to, I'll plug you in the back."

Up to the time of Cleech's death Mahala had been a mother with some trace of human feeling. With the passing of Cleech, that little bit of humanity had passed. She was now unsexed, inhuman, terrible. The men of Rolling Fork were wax in her hands. If pride and the desire to avenge the deaths of Malvin, Asa, and Sile would not make them follow her, fear should drive them.

There was one other man that she wished she had with her. That was her stepbrother, Adam March. But she couldn't have watched him and the Parson both. She meant to kill Adam, anyway.

Mahala cared nothing for Sile and Asa. Their deaths had been a piece of good fortune to her, in that it enabled the Parson, under her direction, to set the Rolling Fork men wild for revenge.

SILENTLY THEY HALTED at the river bank. Silently the boats pulled up. Mahala and the Parson stood and watched

them. She checked them as they climbed aboard. Nine-
ty-three in all.

She and the Parson crossed in the last boat. The night
was made for her dark purpose. Low thunder rumbled and
slow rain was falling. What little noise they would make
would not be noticed.

"Dover Tebo," called Mahala.

The man answered in a low, gruff voice.

"Take ten men and climb the bluff. Get in front of the
house, not too clost, and just watch. Don't do nothing else,
unless somebody tries to come out that way. If they do, get
'em. We don't aim for nary soul that's in that house to get
away."

Dover took his men and disappeared in the darkness.
He knew a way up the bluff, at a wash three hundred yards
south of the Vane House.

Silently, with her shield and buckler before her and her
gun at his unhappy back, Mahala led the way up the bank
of the mill's-tail, across the flat rock, whose bloodstains she
could not see. She caught the toe of her boot on one of the
fishing poles and cursed horribly under her breath. On up
the bank she went, and to the old mill, under cover of the
pitch darkness. Here she stopped by the side of the door
until her men filed into the mill, keeping Parson Chaffin
close by her side all the time.

No one knew better than Mahala that these men were
for the most part honest men and honorable gentlemen,
according to their lights. Frenzied with rage at the death of
four Rolling Fork men, whom they believed to have been
foully murdered by the cattle drover, with the assistance
of Peg Short and Doc Potts, they were going to admin-

ister the only justice that they, and their forbears, had ever known anything about. There were few in that little army that would not have turned back, even then, if they had known the facts, and had realized what Mahala had become while she was in Texas.

Mahala Feeters was not really a product of those hills. She had learned much there in the hills, in her girlhood, but during those eight years while Cleechie sought and found Benton Vane she had graduated in crime, in the toughest cowtowns of frontier Texas. Gun smoke was no novelty to her.

Mahala didn't need all this mob to take three men, and perhaps one woman. Up to the time of Cleech's death, she had meant to clean up the Vanes, then inherit under the law and live like a lady, either in the old Vane House or elsewhere.

Now, in her rage, she meant to destroy the place, leaving no stone on top of another. What money she found she would take back to Texas. A dozen men, yes, half a dozen, with her to lead them, could take the house. After that, the others could destroy the place, burning what would burn, and tearing apart what would not burn.

She now gave her orders in terse whispers. Six besides herself and Parson Chaffin would go to the house.

"As many of you as can, get to them upper mill winders. When I pass the word up that I'm goin' to the house, put so much lead into the upper winders of the house that nobody can shoot out'n 'em and live. Do that for just a minute, then stop. By that time we'll be at the door. If anybody is left alive in that house, we'll 'tend to 'em."

After that they waited in grim silence for the whispered word to be passed up the stair.

IN THE VANE HOUSE five persons still sat in the library, waiting for they knew not what.

"This room, with its windows, is not a safe place, Mr. Vane," began Price Stanley.

"I'm not looking for a safe place!" snapped Vane. "All I want is for some one to try to come in here."

"They won't try to come in at these second-story windows. There is only one way that they can come in from that side, and that is the basement door."

"That's true," said Vane. "Well, we'll go to the hall, and watch that door."

"A bad mistake has been made," old Peg Short growled to the doctor. "Night like this, Price and the girl could got away easy."

"H'm. I know it. Too late now. Have to take our medicine."

Price lost no time getting Myra out of the library. The others followed them into the hall. All attacks had come from the rear of the house, and no one thought of watching the front.

There was no window in the east end of the hall. The broad stair was in the middle, and a closet occupied the space at the back on each side of the stairway. They had not tried to barricade the basement door. In fact, it was not a door, but an open arch that led into an entry. From that entry, doors opened left and right to dining room and kitchen.

Benton Vane, of course, knew every step and turn in the old house. He squatted at the head of the stair, scorning a safe place. The others stood along the rail at each side of the stair.

Out of the dead stillness, save for the drip of water from the eaves, came the crash of a single shot. Bent Vane's guns clicked ominously in the darkness. The next instant a storm of fire broke out. Splintered glass crashed from the windows, while the sound of falling statuary could be plainly heard in the library.

"In with you!" shrieked the rage-hoarsened voice of Mahala, as she pushed Parson Chaffin into the entry ahead of her.

Crash! One of Benton Vane's guns roared. They didn't stop roaring. Alternately they crashed, so close together that the light never died out. Mahala sprang clear, to one side, for she had been in gun fights before. Parson Chaffin went down, with two bullets through his breast, and two others fell on top of him, before they could get out of that infernal entry.

"Come on in!" invited Vane, with a wild laugh. "You're welcome. We'll be glad to have you."

"We're comin'!" Mahala screeched back at him.

"My mistake," said Vane. "I think there is a lady out there," and he laughed heartily, as if it were a great joke.

"Peg," said Doc Potts, in a low tone, "damned if I don't believe the Yankees have come back."

"Reckon not," growled Peg. "I still got my other leg."

A SINGLE SHOT crashed in the entry, at the foot of the stair. The flash showed Benton Vane, squatting at the head of the stair with his guns poised. He didn't fire. In that flash he had seen something. It was a turbaned head and a fiendish face, horribly twisted with rage. He had studied that same straight-lipped face that evening in a portrait while he waited in the library for supper. It was the face of old Anson Vane on the head of Mahala Feeters that he now saw. He never had killed a woman, and he never would kill one, knowingly.

A few moments of silence followed, so tense that Price could hear the beating of Myra's heart as she stood by his side. They were on the side of the stair next to the library door. Peg Short and the doctor were on the other side. The old doctor was calmly holding his guns in his hands, as if waiting for a squirrel to poke his head around a tree. The poking was going to take place pretty soon.

Another storm of bullets swept in at the windows. A Venetian jar that sat on top of the bookshelves went to ruin with a terrific crash.

The firing stopped. Benton Vane's guns began their methodical roaring again, and the hall was full of smoke. Old Doc leaned over the rail and saw his squirrels. They were coming up that basement stair in the very face of death. Vane's guns were empty now, and a dozen hillmen were springing up that stair, over the fallen bodies.

"Go in there and get yo' hands on 'em!" shrieked Mahala. "Come on, you dirty cowards, I'll show you the way!"

Doc's irons began to smoke. Price's two forty-fives joined the roar, with Peg Short doing his bit. That stairway and entry was a seething Hades of fire and lead. No mortal could win through it and live. Such of Mahala's storming party as still lived gave back into the rain-soaked yard, or broke through the doors to dining room and kitchen.

Benton Vane, still squatting at the head of the stair,

reloaded with incredible speed. Down in that dark pit of
Hades, men were groaning in agony and gasping in death.

"Come on, Peg," said Doc Potts, towing Peg Short
around the head of the stair, where Vane still squatted,
waiting for the next move of the enemy.

"Where you goin', Doc?" asked Peg.

"My irons are empty, and I can't see to reload 'em. I'm
goin' to get that ancient matchlock that Bent gave me. It's
on the mantel in the library."

They gained the library, and Doc got his matchlock.
It was an old frontier model forty-five, fully loaded. Doc
had a pocketful of cartridges that Bent had given him.
When the old matchlock was empty, he could try reload-
ing Bent's gun in the dark. Not with the speed of Benton
Vane, perhaps, but he could manage.

"H'm! Feel better now. Lonesome with an empty gun in
a place like this. Damn' lonesome!"

All firing had ceased for the moment. The same cool-
headedness that had caused Price Stanley to keep his men
out of a useless fight with the hill-billies that first afternoon, was actuating the young man now. It was not fear
that was keeping him away from the head of that stair
while the reckless, hot-headed Benton Vane held the spot-
light. The way things were going, Bent's place was going
to be vacant soon.

THE REEK OF new-spilled blood came up the well of that
stair and, mingled with the acrid smoke of burned powder,
created an awful stench. The air was foul and sickening.

No living woman—or man—could stand that atmo-
sphere long. Price began moving Myra along the hall,

toward the little *boudoir*. It would be safer there, and she could at least breathe.

They were about halfway to the door when that stairway erupted again. Price whirled about, with his reloaded guns in his hands, leaving Myra to go on to the comparative shelter of the *boudoir* alone.

Benton Vane was not looking for a safe place. It would have been much better for him if he had. Plenty of bullets were coming up that stairway now, and too many of them were finding Benton Vane. His guns were empty, and as Price reached his side, he fell back and rolled over out of the stream of lead toward the library door, leaving his spot of glory to the young cattle drover.

Mahala's men had emptied their guns, and only a few bullets were coming now, but the blood-maddened hill-billies were coming up the stair in mass formation, slipping in blood and stumbling over their dead. Price's guns began to bark down that terrible stairway.

The head of the attackers crumbled before that blizzard of flame and lead; but when his guns were empty the press at the back was still forcing men on to their death.

Price Stanley struck with his gun, and a giant who had gained the top of the stair toppled back on his fellows.

Followed a moment of wild hand-to-hand fighting, there in the inky darkness.

Price had dropped his guns. He could do no more than catch men and throw them back down the stair. There was no time to do them any great injury.

In the moment when it looked as if Mahala's men would gain the house and end the battle, Old Doc and Peg began spilling lead over the stair rail again, and they gave back into the yard. Out in the yard Mahala was screaming hoarsely:

"Come on, you louts! Rush 'em while their guns are empty! There's only three men—"

"Three hells!" roared a bull voice in the back yard. "Where's Dover Tebo and them fellers? Why don't they come in the front and help take that outfit?"

AT THAT MOMENT the clouds broke and the world was flooded with moonlight. After the inky darkness it seemed light as day. The light showed dimly, even in the smoke-filled hall. Price saw Myra, standing just where he had left her. Like her hotheaded father, she had refused to seek safety while others were in danger. He also saw Benton Vane, sitting up against the wall by the side of the library door, holding his left arm with his right hand. He was down, but not out.

As Price passed him, going toward Myra, he kicked one of his guns toward Price, and said:

"Grab that gun, son! I managed to get it loaded."

Price grabbed up the gun and turned toward Myra again. Peg Short had caught up the thirty-eight rifle that had killed Captain Vane, and found that it still contained cartridges.

"I reckon here's a good stand for us, Peg," said Doc Potts, as he and Peg again took position on each side of the stairway.

Abruptly another attack was launched from the rear, while the front door burst open and half a dozen of Dover Tebo's men fairly catapulted into the hall. Price had a loaded gun, but he did not dare fire, for the men were all about Myra.

He struck once with his gun, and a man went down. They were on him now. Three of the remaining five clinched him, and one jerked away his pistol. The other two had caught Myra.

Crouched against the wall, Benton Vane could see it all, but he was unable to go to the rescue. Old Doc Potts and Peg Short were fighting back the little party that was trying to get up the stair. Myra had screamed just once before a hairy hand had gone over her mouth. Out in the back yard Mahala Feeters had heard that scream and laughed with glee.

"They've got 'em!" she shrieked. "They've got 'em! Come on!"

But when her wing of the army started up that stair, they met plenty of trouble, for Doc and Peg were still on the job. Benton Vane saw Price and Myra in that swirling mass at the front door, and cursed because he was unable to help them. He rose to his feet against the wall and stood impotently watching the struggle, while he gripped his left wrist with his right hand. As he stood watching, with a mingled curse and prayer on his lips, the two struggling masses fell apart.

Boom! Boom! Boom! Boom! Four sullen roars. The Golden Derringers were playing their part in that terrible massacre.

"Damned if they haven't brought up the ordnance at last!" growled Doc Potts. "Look out, Peg! They're goin' to try the stair again."

Doc and Peg went on looking for squirrels, and it was light enough now to see them. No one would get up that stair. After the Golden Derringers had bellowed Price Stanley took just one look to see that Myra was still safe, then went out the front door and fairly into Dover Tebo and his remaining men.

Price had regained his gun and was using it effectively. Dover Tebo and one other man gained the gate and tore along the Old Red Road toward the covered bridge.

The firing ceased suddenly as Price rushed back into the hall and caught Myra in his arms.

"Myra!" called Benton Vane. "My God, child, where are you?"

"Here—here I am!" came a muffled voice.

She was in Price's arms, with her face buried against his shoulder.

"Are you safe?"

"Yes, I'm—I'm all right. I—"

"Oh, I see you are," laughed Vane, still holding his wrist and weaving a little as he stood. "Where's Doc and Peg Short?"

"Here we are, Bent!" called Doc. "We're all right. Peg's still got his other leg, but I'm afraid our hair will be gray if this keeps up. It's awful to be skeered to death."

"Yes," chuckled Vane, "you two old blood-drinkers look scared. What are you doing, holding to the barrel of that rifle, Peg?"

"She clicked on me just as the firing stopped. I didn't have any more cartridges, so I thought I'd just use her for a club, if they came back."

"They won't be back," said Vane. "This fight is over. Who knows where there is a lamp or a candle? I've got to have a light."

13

THE VANE HOUSE SECRET

MORNING PRESENTED A strange scene at the old Vane House. Price and Peg Short had dragged the dead from the hall and stairway, making a heap in the front yard. There were no wounded. They had carried water from the spring and washed down the steps and entry as best they could. Myra, with her skirts tucked up, was wielding a mop in the front hall, where the Golden Derringers had ruined four men beyond repair.

In the bedroom Benton Vane lay on a clean bed, clad in some of his father's clean garments. His minor wounds, a dozen of them, had been dressed. His face was as pale as the pillow on which his head lay, and his blue eyes were unnaturally large in his tanned face.

"I'd better get up and go give those fellows a hand to clean up the mess," he said.

"Lie still, you fool!" growled Dr. Potts. "You lost a couple of gallons of blood last night. If you walk in a week, you'll do well."

"I may not walk, but I'll ride after that herd!" laughed Vane. "That seventy-five thousand dollars puts me ahead of the world, after twenty years of slaving."

Old Peg Short looked into the library. On the floor were bushels of plaster, glass, and fragments of statuary.

One bullet had taken its random way through the open door into the parlor and smashed a cast of Mad Anthony Wayne, who was an ancestor of the Vanes. Peg shook his head at the ruin and walked out the front door.

A man galloped up to the front fence, dismounted, and came in. He was a tall, sun-browned fellow. His batwing chaps flapped and his spurs clinked as he walked. He looked at the dead on the ground, then at old Peg Short.

"Good mornin', pardner. Looks like y'all had a surprise party here last night."

"Yes," said Peg. "The drinks were too strong, and some of the boys didn't go home."

"Looks like it. Is the boss here?"

"Yes. He's in bed."

"No! Old Bent never slept this late in his life."

"He ain't asleep. He's shot some, but you can see him. Come in."

The big spurs trundled through the hall, and Myra watched him in open-eyed wonder.

"Just a scratch, Steve," explained Vane. "Be all right in a day or two. Line the herd out and keep 'em moving. Only forty miles to good grass, but if you don't get 'em to it they'll starve to death. Been living on buck-bushes and sour dock for four hundred miles. I'll overtake you in—"

"You won't overtake anybody for a while," interrupted Dr. Potts.

"Watch me! Is there such a thing as a hospital ambulance in this town, doctor?"

"H'm! Yes. One in my barn. Looks like the first one that was made, though."

"All right, Steve. Take my horse and saddle back with you. When you get back to the outfit, get two mules out of the *remuda* and send them back to me."

"H'm, h'm! Funny place to carry mules, Bent."

"A *remuda* is a band of saddle horses, doctor," smiled Bent Vane.

"Oh! Thought it was a sort of carpet bag. Better make it four mules. Two couldn't pull that thing down hill in dry weather."

"Very well, make it four mules and harness for 'em, Steve. Now go and get that herd moving."

"Just one little thing before I go, boss," said Steve Bradley. "I didn't see anybody movin' about in town as I comes through there, but I saw one fellow that needs treatment."

"What seemed to be the matter with him?"

"He looked like he was awful dead to me."

"H'm! I'm goin' over there directly. I'll put him up where the hogs can't get him."

STEVE WENT ON back to the herd. Dr. Potts went to town and found Adam March lying in the street quite dead.

The exact facts of the passing of Ad March were not known until Dover Tebo told them long afterward. Seeing the fight at the Vane House lost, Dover Tebo and Clytie Perkins had run for it. When they had got to town, Ad March had been standing in front of his store. He had been listening to the battle and wondering what on earth it was all about. He was anxious for news from the front. If the people in the Vane House won, he was in the clear:

he hadn't been in it. If Mahala won, he wanted to know it. He wanted to share in the division of Randall Vane's gold.

"What's happened?" demanded March, as the two men stopped and stood panting for breath.

"Plenty's happened!" snapped Dover Tebo. "You and Old Lige Chaffin, with yo' Lord's anointed and hand of vengeance, has played hell, but—you won't play it no more."

There had been the crash of a single shot from an old Navy, so close that the hair had been scorched at Adam March's temple. Dover and Clytie had got their breath, then passed on over the hog-back.

Dr. Potts found a dozen men in Vaneburg who had been holed up to avoid even the appearance of evil. He cursed them soundly and drove them like dogs. Within an hour, wagons were at the Vane House. They loaded the dead, crossed the bridge, and trundled away down the river to Rolling Fork. There was no danger in the outcasts going to Rolling Fork now. It was a sobered and chastised settlement. Adam March was taken along, and slept with his forbears.

Mahala Chaffin was not found among the dead... Years later there was an old woman who lived in a cabin on one of the draws of Rolling Fork. She was a sort of fortune-teller, and the hill people said she "had a power." She limped badly and was said to have a wooden leg. No one knew any name for her except Aunt Mahala.

IT WAS AFTERNOON of that day. Price, Myra, Peg Short, and Dr. Potts sat in the bedroom with Benton Vane.

"I don't understand this mess yet," said Peg Short.

"I do," replied Benton Vane. "It was a family row."

"Nope. Families fight, but they don't fight that way just for fun. That gang was after Randall Vane's gold."

"After what?"

"Randall Vane's gold. Everybody knowed Randall sold his niggers just before the war and buried the gold money. Everybody knows your father lived here ever since the war, and all the money he ever made was a little pasturage from that clover field."

Benton Vane laughed long and loud, then he wiped his eyes and said:

"Peg, that's the best joke I've heard since I left Texas! I'll tell you what became of Randall Vane's gold. In the first place, there never was as much of it as people thought. Grandfather sold his slaves on the block, and bidding for slaves wasn't very brisk just then. Randy was a bit of a stepper when he was away from grandmother, and he made a trip to New Orleans to sell those niggers. What with poker on the steamboat, some parties in the Creole City, and a lot of white velvet carpet and other fool gimcracks that he brought back here, he reduced that wonderful lot of gold considerably.

"Then, after father went away to the war, and grandfather was dead, I took the key away from the old colored woman, Aunt Dilsey, and helped myself. If you think a fool boy can't get away with some money in four years, just try one. When father came back here, there wasn't enough gold left in that old vault to fill a tooth. I tried to make it up to him. I've sent him money to live on and to pay his taxes for twenty years."

"Then why did he always keep that door locked?" asked Myra.

"Habit, I suppose. It was the strong box of the family. I guess there's a stack of Anson and Randall Vane's old account books and things like that, but gold—no."

"Then why did grandmother want the key?" asked Myra. "I'm sure she hunted it all the last day she lived, was hunting it when she was killed."

"Maybe she thought there was gold there. Maybe Mahala and her rabble thought there was. I don't."

"I wish I had that key," said Myra. "I'll never be satisfied until I know."

"H'm! Key, did you say? An old brass key. H'm! Forgot about that. Fell out of Cap'n Vane's pocket when I was takin' his wet clothes off. Put it in my pocket. Forgot it. Here it is."

Dr. Potts held out a worn brass key for inspection.

"That's it," said Benton Vane, taking the worn key and looking at it. "That key has been used about a hundred years. Here, Myra. Take it. You and Price go look for that gold. If you find it you can split it between you—if you want to split.

"By the way, Myra," he added. "I guess the Vane House here—what's left of it—belongs to you."

Myra looked about her at the rubbish-strewn rooms which had been like a prison for her before they were turned into a shambles. She shuddered.

"No," she said decisively. "I'm going away. I never want to set foot in this house again."

Price took the brass key, and he and Myra went to explore the treasure room.

"BENTON, THAT PRICE STANLEY is a powerful fine boy."

"Yes," smiled Benton Vane. " 'Right smaht figger of a

man,' as old man Randy used to say. Myra could do a lot worse… While they are gone, I've got something to tell you two. Myra doesn't want this old house, nor I, and it wouldn't bring four bits now. Maybe the land will be worth something some day. Still, I was born here, and I hate to see it go to ruin. If you two will come and live here, I'll give you a thousand dollars to put some windows in the house and make it fit to live in. It's yours as long as you want it."

"H'm, h'm! Good fishin' in that little blue hole. Plenty squirrels in the bottom. Dacy Blodgett and his wife could live in the nigger house and cook for us. H'm. What say, Peg?"

"Long ways to walk to my shop on this wooden leg."

"Let your shop go to the devil!" snapped Vane. "Rent the clover patch to drovers, make that lazy devil of a Dacy Blodgett farm the river field."

"Shore, shore!" said Peg. "Hadn't thought of that. Suits me, Doc, suits me fine. Tired peggin' shoes, anyway."

The two old fellows went out to look over their new home and see how much work it would take to fix up the tumbledown stable that stood across the Red Road by the clover patch.

After a long time, Price and Myra returned to Vane's room. There were cobwebs in Myra's hair, and a new light in her eyes. They walked up to Vane's bed and stopped. Benton Vane appeared not to notice that they were holding hands.

"Find any gold, Myra?" he asked.

"No, sir, but— You tell him, Price."

"Feel cheated, don't you, Price?"

"No, sir! We didn't find any gold, but Myra and I—
we—I—I want to ask you—"

"That's all right, son," smiled Benton Vane, "just as soon
as we can find a preacher and a license. I'm mighty proud
of the way this has turned out, proud of you and proud of
Myra.

"I have something to tell you two. Myra hasn't had a
square deal in life, but I didn't mean for it to be that way.
All this mystery and wondering about her has been need-
less. It was on account of my father's living the life of a
recluse since the Confederacy was lost. The whole story is
that I went away from this old place to make my fortune in
Texas. I had no more than landed there when I met Myra's
mother. She was a daughter of a fine old Texas family, a
family that any one might be proud to be connected with.
We loved each other, and were married on the day we first
met, so I can't find fault with you two for doing almost the
same thing.

"Within the year, Myra was born, and soon afterward her mother died. The world had gone black for me.
I supposed I would drift about a while, then come back
to Vaneburg. I loved my baby girl, but I couldn't take her
with me. I wanted her to be raised as the Vanes had been
raised, and her mother's people didn't have much money.
So I decided to send her to my father.

"When I started drifting I soon learned that the boy was
gone out of me, and I didn't enjoy the wild life any more.
There was plenty of opportunity, and I became a ranch-
man. For twenty years I slaved to become a cattle king, and
I made the grade.

"I didn't forget you, Myra. I was always thinking that

I would come back to see you, and that my money would make you a little princess. The trouble was I always thought of you as a little girl, and I could hardly grasp it all when I saw you a grown young woman, and in love with a man… I said a man, and I meant it. Drover, I take off my hat to you. I'll be glad to call you son. I'm satisfied. The years slipped by, while I was busy… You had better run along, now, and see if you can rustle something to eat."

There was a look of pride in Vane's eyes as he watched them leave the room, hand in hand.

The great lumbering old ambulance, drawn by four mules with Price's Kentucky saddler led behind, drove away from the Vane house next morning and took the old Red Road north. Two white-haired old men stood in the road and watched until it disappeared around the bend of the road, then listened to the clatter of hoofs on the old covered bridge until the sound died out.

"H'm, h'm! Gone. Fine young fellow as I ever saw. Prettiest gal in the State. Never saw one I'd do that much fightin' for. But then, I'm a bachelor. H'm. Come on. Let's load our irons and go squirrel huntin'."

ONE SUNNY MORNING a week later that same old ambulance jolted and jangled along the road far out on the rolling, blue-stem prairie country. On the front seat sat Mr. and Mrs. Sterling Price Stanley. On the back seat was Benton Vane. The Kentucky saddler was still tailing along behind.

From the crest of a ridge they could see the blue timber of the Missouri River far in the distance, across the sweeping prairie. To their left lay a pasture of a thousand acres of native blue-stem. On a hill, in a grove of trees, stood a big white house, with green blinds and a red brick chimney at each end.

"Home, Myra," said Price. "Our home. I'm the only child in our family, and they'll never let me leave."

"And I'll have a mother!" said Myra, with a little choke of joy.

A man on a big Kentucky saddler rode up out of a deep hollow ahead of them and came on to meet them. He was a giant-framed old man whose hair was iron-gray. Dave Baker had come in with the thousand cattle the day before. He had told his story. Banks Stanley had said nothing, but when morning came he had buckled on his guns and started to hunt his boy. Now he found him almost at his door.

The ambulance stopped, and Banks Stanley pulled up beside it.

"Hello, dad!" greeted Price. "This is my wife and your new daughter, Myra, and my father-in-law, Benton Vane."

"Huh! Dave said you stopped to help somebody. Looks to me like you helped yourself a-plenty. Glad to know you, Mr. Vane."

"Fine grass over there," said Benton Vane. "Belong to you?"

"Yes."

"I've got five thousand cattle coming on. Be here about night. Like to bed 'em on that to-night. Pay you what's right." Benton Vane had forgotten everything but his cattle.

"What on earth are you going to do with that many cattle?" asked Banks Stanley.

"They're sold to Captain Jimmy Jones."

"Oh, they are? Let 'em eat Jimmy Jones's own grass, then. It's right across the lane."

The ambulance rolled on down the road to the big red gate.

"I've heard of the blue-stem country," said Myra. "I've always thought of it as a sort of heaven—and it is."

"Any place is heaven where you are," said Price, as he swung the four mules through the home gate.

www.ingramcontent.com/pod-product-compliance
Lightning Source LLC
Chambersburg PA
CBHW030529020726
47494CB00004B/1286